PLOWED

KRISTEN LUCIANI
& REBECCA MANUEL

Plowed
By Kristen Luciani and Rebecca Manuel

Cover Design by Rebecca Manuel and Jena Brignola of Bibliophile Productions, www.bibliophileproductions.com

Editing by Megan Saperstein, authorsaperstein@aol.com

Formatting by Champagne Formats
www.champagneformats.com

ISBN 13: 978-0-9907575-6-6
ISBN 10: 0-9907575-6-0

PLOWED

ONE

SIX MONTHS. TWO WORDS THAT HAD chilled Daxton to the core from the second they were uttered. Certainly not ones that could make his near-flaccid cock any harder, despite the pair of collagen-infused lips clamped with determination - sucking, pulling and tugging to no avail. He clenched the arms of the plush leather recliner, as his eyes squeezed shut in an attempt to force images of his family's tear-streaked faces far from his mind when they'd received the prognosis.

Jase had only been eighteen. Eighteen! What kind of God gives a kid an inoperable brain tumor and allows it to ravage his body, decimating his once-muscular frame down to nothing more than ashen skin and brittle bones? Brain Cancer. A fucking death sentence. The pain of such a loss ran deep into the crevices of Daxton's fractured soul. A world without Jase had been inconceivable. The guy always lit up a room with his mega-watt smile and equally charged personality. Nothing was ever doomed; there was always a silver lining. Glass half full and all that crap. He'd been a glittering diamond in a world of coal.

But despite all the positivity Jase could muster, reality bore its ugly-ass head, claiming his young and formerly vibrant life. Daxton's baby brother and best friend was gone, forever. Days turned into months and shit never got easier, no matter what people said. There were three means of escape – booze, sex, and music – but they were temporary. And when the buzz wore off, grief always prevailed.

"Come on, Daxy. Why can't you get hard?" The whining voice grated on his nerves, blunted as they were from the excess of whiskey. "I wanna make you come. Tell me what to do so I can get you off." Why couldn't she just shut the hell up? And when would the toxic thoughts streaming through his foggy mind finally stop?

Show time was in two hours and here he was, hung over from day-drinking, and getting sucked off by some bleached blonde backup singer named…Brandi? Brianne? Bambi? What the hell ever. Typical behavior for an insensitive asshole with the emotional stability of Jell-O. At least, that was the commonly held opinion of his father, legendary rock god Tyler Cole. Performing on the anniversary of Jase's death was nothing short of a mortal sin in his book. Not that Daxton had ever been able to make him happy or proud. Nope, that was all reserved for Jase.

Long, hot pink-lacquered nails trailed down his thighs, cupping his balls, kneading them with urgency. But his heart was too empty, and his mind was too full to cooperate with the valiant efforts.

He pushed her away. "Stop."

The blonde's eyes widened. Her mouth fell open, his cock slipping from her still-pursed lips. "What did you say?"

"I said, enough. Just get dressed and go."

"I thought you wanted to—"

He raked a hand through his longish-dark hair. "I'm not into it anymore."

"You're a real asshole, you know that?" Blondie jumped to her feet, hands on her hips, clad only in a red lacy bra and matching thong. Her body was tight and her tits were huge, but his brain refused to provide him any bit of release.

"Yeah, that's one I've heard a few times before." He stood, zipping up his low-slung black jeans. More alcohol was a necessity. His pounding head did nothing to deter him from grabbing another highball glass and filling it with the amber-colored liquid.

"I wasted the past half hour on my knees, and you're still limp as a freaking spaghetti noodle. Not like you bothered to return the favor. So much for your reputation. Sex god, my fucking ass. You can't even get it up!" The girl shimmied back into her obscenely short pleather mini-dress and flipped him off. "Fuck you, Daxton Cole. You have no idea what you're missing."

He blinked several times, his half-hooded eyes focused on her overly made up face. Her lips twisted into a nasty grimace, brown eyes so heavily lined she resembled a raccoon, a really skanky one at that. "I guess my cock's just not interested. He's obviously got better taste than I do."

"Drop dead, dickhead. And break a leg. Literally!" She stormed out of the dressing room. The door slammed so hard, the walls shook. Or maybe that was the booze talking. He downed the rest of the Jim Beam and tucked in his ear buds, *Dream On* by Aerosmith looping on repeat. It had been Jase's song of choice in those final days. Listening to it was such bittersweet torture; a never-ending internal battle between the need to feel closer to his brother versus the subsequent emotional assault that commenced each time Steven Tyler's voice filled his ears. Christ, he was like a Ferrari headed straight into a tree, clocking a hundred and fifty. A fucking disaster of epic proportions, cruising toward the inevitable crash.

"Your skirt is too short, Sara. Remember the fingertip rule!"

Her mother's normally crisp voice, edged with judgment, echoed in Sara's mind. "Too short" was a gross understatement. Bending over without flashing the world was damn near impossible, and if she were back in Minnesota, the view from behind would have gotten her hauled in for indecent exposure. Outside her socialite, stick-up-the-ass, bubble-of-a-life back home, it was perfectly acceptable to flaunt butt cheeks, cellulite and all. But not for the only trophy daughter of Mayor Dirk Russell and his wife, Susan, the reigning Ice Queen of Grand Falls. They'd always made it abundantly clear that Sara lived in their world, not the other way around. How ironic that most of the time, they barely acknowledged her existence at all. Yet another reason why they'd vehemently insisted she flee after…everything.

Sara squeezed her eyes shut to block out the horrifying images, shrugging off the useless guilt that haunted her daily. If she let the events of that fateful night grab hold of her, if she allowed those chilling memories to percolate for even one second… No! Tonight was too important. She finally had a chance to break free, to escape that life, to figure out who the hell she really was. And right now, she was *late*.

Her legs moved through the corridors as quickly as the four-inch heels would allow. Jeez, she'd only been wearing the knee-length suede boots for about thirty minutes and already her ankles were ready to collapse. How did girls make it look so easy? And why didn't she practice walking in them a little longer, like Casie, her first friend in Houston, had suggested? Kitten heels were about as close to daring as she'd ever gotten back home. Anything higher was frowned upon, along with everything fun and exciting. One of her heels caught on the carpet as she scurried toward her destination. She stumbled forward, managing to land cleanly against a nearby wall. Smooth, real smooth. A quick glance around confirmed that nobody saw, nor cared. Anonymity. Exactly what she wanted.

Her wardrobe no longer screamed conservative politician's daughter, thanks to Casie. She'd become her new friend's pet project from day one. No way could she sport her signature floral frocks as a junior publicist for Zenith Public Relations. And her Keds? Out with the next morning's trash. To be taken seriously in this business, you had to look the part. At least, that was Casie's mantra. But all the trampy clothes and makeup in the world couldn't erase the blackness that stained Sara's soul.

She caught a glimpse of her reflection in a large mirrored wall as she scampered down one of the hallways in the underbelly of the City Center Arena. Her top revealed just enough, courtesy of the push-up bra she'd scored from Victoria's Secret the day before. A hint of boob, the rest left to the imagination. If only her parents could see how conservative she looked next to the likes of the other interns milling about.

Stopping outside the large black door, Sara plastered a smile on her face. Her hand gripped the handle, goose bumps popping up along her exposed flesh. She pushed open the door, light illuminating the expansive room. With a few quick blinks, her heart dropped to her stomach with absolutely nothing to cushion the landing, save for a few shreds of lettuce from the salad she'd choked down hours earlier.

Empty. Not a soul occupied the space.

Oh crap. Where the heck was everyone? She checked her clipboard and then the number on the door. They matched, so what changed? And why didn't anyone tell her? If she didn't find them, if they didn't make it to their--

The cell phone stuck in the band of her skirt vibrated. Crap. Someone was about to get fired and her name began with 'S.'

"Suri, we need Jimmy Sixx like, yesterday. Where the hell are they?"

"Casie!" Forget the annoying nickname that her friend

insisted on using because Sara was much too plain-Jane for a publicist in the music industry.

A cackle sounded over the line. "Sorry, but Sara doesn't really fit this new you. Suri is way cooler, don't you think?"

"Forget the nickname. Jimmy Sixx isn't here!" Perspiration beaded on the back of her neck.

"What are you talking about? The press is climbing the walls!"

"The room is empty. Oh my God, where could they be? Did someone move them? Are they—?"

"Just calm down and listen to me. *Ask* someone, for chrissakes."

"Don't swear at me! I'm freaking out here!"

"Fuck the language, choir girl. Find the damned band before your hot little ass gets terminated."

"Okay, okay!"

Each breath became more and more shallow until it felt like all the oxygen from her lungs was squeezed out. A paper bag might do her good at that moment. Her eyes darted around, her throat tightening even more, if that was even possible. Everyone was dressed in black, and most people had long hair – guys and girls alike. Piercings and tattoos were ubiquitous. Jimmy Sixx could be anywhere and she would have absolutely no idea if one of the band members came up and bit her on the nose. Maybe it would have been smart to Google them after all. It was, quite literally, like trying to find four needles in a haystack. Not happening without some kind of miracle. And girls like her didn't qualify.

Man, she could've used a Diet Coke, although caffeine

probably wasn't a smart thing to ingest when her heart was racing like a thoroughbred trying to win the Triple Crown. She wiggled her toes in the too-tight boots and took off, headed toward... oh right, where the hell was she *going*? Wandering around aimlessly wasn't getting her any closer to finding the four faceless guys she'd been ordered to represent. Such a simple assignment, yet she'd already managed to royally screw it up. It was the new beginning she'd hoped for, a chance to rid herself of the ugliness, to breathe without constantly peeking over her shoulder. Dammit, she had to pull it together and find the freaking band before—

"Ahh!" A metal grate on the floor held her boot heel captive, but her body gave no regard to the imprisoned foot. "Watch out!" The force yanked her out of the boot, sending her careening into an unfortunate passer-by who didn't so much as lift an eyebrow at her shrieks of panic. He hadn't even looked up as she flew through the air. Nope, it wasn't until she was plastered on top of him, soaked from head to now-bare toe in whatever the hell sticky, sugary concoction he'd been carrying that she got any bit of a reaction. A chill zipped through her. He shifted with a loud groan, hands settling on her back. Dark eyes narrowed on her chest, a slow, sexy smile lifting the corners of his deliciously full, kissable lips.

Her eyes dropped to the ample cleavage spilling out of her fabulous new bra, dangerously close to that sinful mouth. A gasp escaped. *Oh good Lord, please let this be a dream...*

He pulled out a black ear bud. Perfectly white teeth blinded her as his sensuous mouth curled upward. "Wow, a front row seat at a wet t-shirt contest? I guess the press can wait a few more minutes."

TWO

T HEY WEREN'T GREEN. TOO MANY FLECKS
of brown and gold glimmered in the depths. Swirls
of color swam into focus – rays of yellow and blue
blending to form a hazel gaze; they were so captivating,
so hypnotic. Words temporarily evaded him...but, were
they really twinkling? Or was he that fucked up from the
whiskey he'd just downed?

Some kind of scent awakened his dulled senses... it
was fruity, maybe raspberry? Mmm, sweet and juicy, much
like the rack on the fallen angel plastered on top of his very
aroused body. Clearly, the excess of booze hadn't blunted
the sensations rocketing into every extremity.

Long, toned legs straddled him, and a perfect-
ly-too-short denim skirt was dangerously close to exposing
the part of her that was still covered. *Barely.*

"Oh my gosh, I'm so sorry!" The girl recoiled, clutching the bare skin now glistening with droplets of Jim Beam. "I can't believe I just did that. God, I'm such a freaking spaz! Are you okay?"

He licked his lips, fighting back a grin. A deep red flush colored her cheeks. Her mortification was fucking adorable. What he wouldn't do for a chance to drag his tongue across that soft skin, lapping up every last taste. "You definitely got my attention. Pretty aggressive move. Most women prefer *me* on top."

Her mouth fell open, jaw pretty much crashing to the floor. "*Excuse* me?"

"You just plowed into me. I'm thinking I should return the favor."

"Trust me, I couldn't be less interested." Blonde hair hung around her heart-shaped face in sticky strands, slapping against her back as she leapt to her feet, panic etched into her features. "Great, I'm freaking soaked!"

He raised himself onto his elbows to get a closer look. Damn, his hands itched to run over those smooth, creamy thighs, muscles flexing as she straightened. A quick glance confirmed her ass was as bitable as he'd imagined. "Not quite, but I can definitely help out in that department."

"You're a disgusting pig!" Her plump pink lips pursed and her nostrils flared. He'd finally struck a chord, and man, did he want to strum her strings. She had some fire in her. *Nice. That could be fun later.*

"Ouch." He clutched a hand to his heart. "If you didn't want the attention, you should have worn a different shirt."

A loud gasp escaped from those lips, the ones he wanted

wrapped tightly around his now-aching cock. That's when the death look smoked him like a bug under a magnifying glass. "How classy of you to notice. It's probably the only action you'll get tonight anyway. *Roadie.*"

"True. I guess I got a little overexcited. It's been awhile. You know how us roadies never get any. But if you change your mind…"

"In your dreams." She scurried around him, squinting at the floor, giving him more than a glimpse of what lay beneath her skirt, if it could even qualify as that. *Bend over just a little bit more… just a tiny little bit…*

"I'm not so sure about that since you're not running away."

Her eyes blazed as she straightened. Oh, Christ, there was a lot of rage bubbling beneath the surface, and she was about to unleash it all over him…. or rather, who she thought he was, the roadie. Anonymity was awesome.

"You are positively vile."

"Does that mean I can't have your number?"

"Yeah, because I've already got yours. Loser." She grabbed her lone boot and stomped toward the nearest ladies' room, door slamming behind her.

Dammit, that perfect ass had just slipped right through his fingers. With a deep sigh, he popped in his ear buds and dragged himself to his feet. How crazy was it that he couldn't get it up for a hot, naked chick actively sucking him off, but for the girl who looked at him like he was no better than the scum on the bottom of her designer boots, instant hard-on? He raked a hand through his hair, a smile playing at his lips. Yeah, maybe that was just what he needed.

Sara gripped the edges of the sink, breaths expelling in short, desperate gasps. The nerve of that jerk! She jammed her foot back into the boot, shivering in the air-conditioned room. It was definitely because of the sopping wet fabric clinging to her, not from the feeling of his hands skimming her drenched skin. Forget the tingles that scooted down her back under the spell of his chocolately gaze. What the heck was wrong with her, having these thoughts about a guy who'd wanted nothing other than to cop a free feel? Blech!

The temptation to peek at her reflection was too much to resist. A freaking train wreck stared back, one resembling a drowned rat. And what had been in that glass? She smelled like a barfly drunk off its ass, but at least her eye makeup was still intact. Thank goodness for waterproof mascara. Yep, there was the silver lining. Too bad the rest of her looked like she'd won first place in said wet t-shirt contest. She pulled a hair tie off her wrist and wrapped the sticky strands into a low knot. A quick look at her watch made her yelp. Late, as in so late she could pick up her walking papers on the way to the pressroom late. And oh yeah, she still hadn't found the band. Just a minor detail. *Okay, Sara, just keep calm and... oh, Lord.* A hasty pat down followed by a panicked full body check confirmed her iPhone was gone. *Darn it!* Just like everything else that had been good in her life, she'd managed to screw this up, too. There was no bailout plan. She was on her own, for better or worse. And judging from the evidence, it was most definitely *worse*.

Tears pooled in her eyes and she swiped at them. This was her new life, her clean slate, away from the noxious existence she'd fled. *Can't go back home, can't be that person anymore.* With a stomp of her foot, she gritted her teeth. No! This could be fixed. It had to be salvageable. She'd buried her pathetically weak alter ego the second she stepped on the plane and her resurrection had never been a consideration.

A deep breath did little to calm her thundering pulse. She yanked open the bathroom door, eyes scouring the crowded corridor. It was almost show time and the buzz generated by all of the frantic activity reminded her not to blow this chance. Crew members shouted into walkie talkies. Equipment littered the space. Too bad she didn't have time to enjoy the rush. Just find the phone and the band, and then get the hell to the pressroom. Those were the objectives and nothing would stop—

"I found this on the floor where you pummeled me. Yours?"

The deep, gravelly voice reverberated through her. She spun around and grabbed the phone he was dangling. "Shouldn't you be working? The show starts in less than an hour. Or are you just paid to harass people who are trying to get their jobs done?"

"Says the girl who climbed me like Mount Everest and didn't even bother to ask if I enjoyed it." His eyes glimmered in the overhead light. "Tsk, tsk. Where are you manners?"

"You are so infuriating!"

14

"Yeah, but check this out. I'm also thoughtful." He tossed her a concert t-shirt. "You smell a little like you've been hitting the bottle. *Hard.*"

The handsy roadie actually *helped* her? She bit her lower lip. Maybe he wasn't such a douchebag. "Um, thank you…" Wait a minute. An extra small? Seriously? So much for not being a sleaze. Her eyes narrowed. "You know, I really hope you don't think—" The iPhone in her hand buzzed. "Oh my gosh, Casie, please tell me you found them!"

"Relax, it's all good. Everyone is on the way to the pressroom. You're off the hook."

Saved! A sigh of relief escaped Sara's lips. "Thank God! I'm not fired!"

"Not yet. But get your ass down here pronto. I don't know how much longer I can cover for you."

"Thank you so much, Casie! I don't know what I'd do—"

"Yeah, yeah. Just buy me a beer later." Casie snickered. *Click.*

A wide smile spread across Sara's face, then faded almost as quickly as it appeared. Where the heck was the pressroom? What if it was on the other side of the arena? She'd never make it there before the band. The hyperventilating began again and her throat tightened with each passing second. Who could she—

She caught a sexy smirk in her periphery. *Oh, hell no…*

"You okay, Princess? That look makes me think you're about to jump me again. You know, out of gratitude this time."

Her hands flew to her temples, but what choice did

she have? The guy might be a crude jerkoff but there was a press pass hanging around his neck... a neck that led to a half-exposed and very muscular chest. Not sure why a roadie would be wearing one of those, but who cared? She was desperate and he obviously had nothing better to do than taunt her. And find her a shirt so she didn't make a complete fool of herself on the first day. That alone was worth a bunch of points.

He straightened, his black button-down falling open even more, giving her a full glimpse of what lay beneath. Her fingers twitched, eyes raking over his tanned skin. Oh sweet Lord, how she wanted to trace every single indentation. Ahhh! Who *was* she?

"Go change. I'll wait."

She channeled her inner Flash and was back in seconds, still somewhat sticky, and extremely aroused. Her neck strained when he approached, a full head taller than she was. At least 6'2", with a tight, taut body, whose close proximity made her knees wobble. *Remember the objectives!* Objectives? Um... yeah, press room!

"So you're in some kind of rush to get there?"

"Yes." She tapped her foot against the tiled floor, forcing her eyes in every direction but his. "So, you know, anytime you're *ready.*"

The belly of the arena was a labyrinth of the most complex design. She'd have been lost within seconds if not for her tour guide. Keeping up was nearly impossible, but that left time to ogle the view. Yum. Minutes later, they'd reached their destination. She drew in a deep breath. Time to kick some ass.

With an exaggerated wink, he held open the door. She charged past, spotting Casie in the corner with three tall guys. Definitely rocker-types, dressed from head-to-toe in black, wearing sunglasses, low-slung jeans, and deep scowls. Yep, this must be Jimmy Sixx. Except…

"Sara! Come here so you can meet the band. The conference will be starting in about five minutes. Cooper, Finn, Liam, this is Sara Russell, our newest junior publicist."

"It's so great to meet you all." She smiled as the introductions were made, trying to mask her confusion. All accounts stated there were four members of Jimmy Sixx. Was it possible one had defected? Dammit, she really needed to spend more time online. Resisting Google would crush her newfound career aspirations faster than she could pull up Chrome.

"Hold that thought. You may change your tune in a second." Liam grinned past her. "It's about time you showed up, man. The press won't wait forever. Not even for someone as pretty as you."

"Sorry, I don't—" Sara's brow furrowed as her eyes followed Liam's line of sight. Holy mother of God.

Deep-set eyes glittered down on her as those familiar, delectable lips lifted into a mischievous grin, revealing a dimple in his left cheek. She swallowed hard, almost choking on the golf ball-sized lump in her throat. The *roadie*?

"Sara, this is Daxton Cole, lead singer for Jimmy Sixx."

I T WAS IMPOSSIBLE NOT TO CRACK A SMILE. The blonde couldn't have looked more shocked if she'd suddenly lost all of her clothes and was standing in front of the press in her birthday suit. And judging from the way those clothes clung to her luscious curves, it was definitely a vision that would have Daxton pumping his hand later.

Sara's green eyes, wide with confusion, focused on him. Words still hadn't emerged, but her perfect, pink lips pursed, patiently awaiting sounds to push forth. For a girl who'd had plenty to say just a few minutes earlier, she was currently rendered mute. So self-righteous, yet demure at the same time. It was an insanely, not to mention refreshingly, hot combination, considering all of the desperate, fame-seeking groupies flooding his inner circle. They didn't know the meaning of the word demure. Probably couldn't pronounce it, either.

"It's very nice to meet you, Sara." Peeling his eyes away was futile. An aura of innocence surrounded her, despite the skimpy outfit and snarky tongue. *Fuck yeah, that tongue.* He could think of a million and one things she could be doing with that tongue and none of them required her to utter a single syllable.

"Nice to meet you, too." Her cheeks flushed a deep shade of pink, eyes averted. So unlike the normal prospects, girls who knew all too well who he was and what he could get them. But this chick really had no clue, which meant no agenda. That alone made him semi-hard. How fucking sad.

Merrick Quinn, the band manager and his best friend, headed toward them, squeezing through the crowds of reporters and photographers with his cell phone in hand. He was loud, inappropriate more often than not, and kind of a prick, but he'd been the one by Daxton's side through… everything. "Okay, guys. You know the drill. The press gets fifteen minutes for questions, and then we're out. The opening band is taking the stage in five, and I don't want any delays tonight."

"The lead singer from Smeared Lipstick is fucking hot. I'd like to tap that. Like, tonight." Finn snickered.

Liam yawned and stretched his arms overhead. "Didn't you already hit it? Your recovery rate is impressive, man."

"Jealous?"

"Negative. Just fucking tired. We've been in and out of cities for the past two weeks with no break. I'm ready to hibernate for the next few days."

"Strap yourself in, Liam. We've got another few weeks to go after the hiatus, and Smeared Lipstick is our new opener. So if Finn doesn't get his tonight, there's always tomorrow." Merrick snickered. "Okay, let's get this press conference rolling."

The press box was standing room only. Flashbulbs popped as the photogs snapped seemingly incessant streams of pictures, something Daxton had never gotten used to, even after all these years. He'd lived under a microscope his whole life as Tyler Cole's son. And Tyler hadn't taken too kindly to Daxton's decision to jumpstart his own career. Stepping out of the shadows, putting his talents on display for the world to see...it was the only way for Daxton to establish his own self-worth after all the years of being told he wasn't good enough, that he wasn't Jase. And the press had been all over Daxton like maggots on rotting meat. The limelight surrounding his father dimmed substantially, essentially leaving him in darkness, as Daxton steadily climbed the charts. His success was just another sore point in their otherwise fractured relationship, as welcome as a fart in an elevator.

He gritted his teeth. Damn his father for not ever giving a shit. Maybe he wouldn't be such an emotional train wreck if his dad had focused even a modicum of attention on him over the years, instead of tearing him down every chance he got. Tyler's top priority was always Tyler. Jase had been second. Daxton didn't rate.

His chest tightened at the thought of Jase. Being on the road was the most effective distraction. He didn't want to think about what would happen when the last note was sung. They had a few days between this show and the final leg of the tour, and being alone with his thoughts and feelings of inadequacy always made for a very drunken, hazy hiatus. Too bad he couldn't ever channel that angst into his songs. He might not be so fucked in the head if he let it all out in his music. But maybe he didn't want to let anyone in. Maybe he didn't want the world to see the ugliness that surrounded him on a daily basis.

A row of plush leather chairs that faced the press awaited them. The guys huddled around Merrick and Asya, their senior publicist, for last minute prep before taking their seats. But Daxton was only-half listening. His singular focus was on Sara, who was standing a few feet away with Casie. His eyes raked over her long, toned legs. Hard to believe only a few short minutes ago, she'd been sprawled on top of him, breathless and dripping wet. Circumstances were far from ideal, but his curiosity had been piqued. A growing ache in his groin compromised his ability to think straight...or at all, for that matter. It was a well-timed diversion. He needed to get his head screwed on, to forget all of the bullshit, if only for a few hours.

"So you're not a roadie." Sara inched toward him, tugging on a large, silver hoop earring. He focused on her bright white teeth, imagining them chewing on his lip, and anywhere else she wanted to nibble...A pink flush inched down her neck, drawing his attention to the fullness of her pert breasts.

"Would you like me better if I was?"

"I'm not being paid to like you. I'm being paid to salvage your reputation." The corners of her luscious lips curled into a smile. "Count me out of your little games. I appreciate you saving my ass with the t-shirt, but please don't think that'll make me fawn all over you."

"Well, you've already fallen all over me. Maybe not because of my fame, but—"

She shook her head, long blonde tendrils bouncing over her shoulders. "Sorry. Not happening."

"You should give me another shot. Maybe I'm not the guy you think I am."

"As your new junior publicist, my job is to prove exactly that to the rest of the world. And anyway, I have a boyfriend; one who doesn't have an ego the size of an arctic land mass."

"You're getting all geographical now. That's hot."

Sara rolled her bright green eyes heavenward. "I'm sure your groupies are incapable of formulating complete sentences. No wonder you're so impressed."

"That doesn't say much for me."

"It says a heck of a lot."

"Dax, you want to join the rest of the group? We're starting." Merrick nudged him toward the single empty seat.

He sank into the chair, his mind reeling. A fire ignited deep within him, intense heat snaking its way throughout his extremities. Desire bubbled beneath the surface, his arms twitching to grab her, to feel her body flush against his, to pound into—

Casie clapped her hands, interrupting the very carnal thought permeating his mind. "Thanks to all of you for joining us tonight. We'll be taking questions for the next fifteen minutes. Who's first?"

Seemed like every hand shot up. With all the press coverage on Jimmy Sixx in the past months, it was hard to imagine they were not out of material. It was going to be a long fifteen minutes. And man, did his cock ache.

Sara's heart thudded with the speed of the camera flashes. The pounding was so loud, she was certain it could be heard above the din in the press box. So forceful, she feared it might explode through her chest at any given moment.

Daxton Cole. Roadie turned Jimmy Sixx front man. Lead singer, currently turning her knees to rubber under the weight of his brooding stare. The press had been peppering him with questions since the conference started, and he'd barely acknowledged any of them. He doled out one word answers, if they were lucky. Most questions were deflected to the rest of the band. It seemed like nothing could divert his attention. That penetrating gaze never wavered, pinning her to the spot, trapped like a rat in a cage with no exit option.

"Dax, is there any truth to the rumors about you and Gia Lourdes?"

The corners of his lips curled into a sexy grin. "I don't like to kiss and tell."

Sweet Lord, that smile was swoon-worthy. A tiny chill shimmied down her spine as his dimple deepened. Beads of perspiration popped up on the back of her neck, despite the chilled air blowing up her skirt. And Lord, did that area need some cooling off.

"Will you attend your dad's upcoming wedding to model Layla Reynolds?"

Cue the record scratch sound effect. No pun intended. Looked like someone finally struck a chord - the *wrong* one - judging by the instant change in Daxton's demeanor. The expression on his chiseled face darkened, like a black cloud eclipsing the sun on a bright spring day. His eyes, no longer focused squarely on Sara's; it narrowed in the reporter's direction, mouth twisting into a grimace. "No comment."

The rest of the band jumped on the remaining questions. Daxton never uttered another word. Gone was the cocky, flirtatious rock god. He turned away from the cameras, from the curious stares, a forlorn look replacing the sexy smirk he'd worn only moments before. An unfamiliar fluttering sensation erupted when his pained expression navigated back to her. Disappointment, rejection, anger… she saw it all. Maybe he'd chosen to let the façade crumble. Or maybe she just recognized those emotions all too well because she'd experienced them herself.

"You look incredibly sexy right now, but I'm counting the minutes until I can get you out of those clothes."

She jumped, a warm flush heating her cheeks. "Eli, what are you doing here?"

"I've got some news. We'll have to celebrate. *Later.*" He grasped her hips, his lips grazing her ear. "Just wait until I get you home."

"Okay, no more questions. Thanks for your time this evening. Enjoy the show." Casie flipped off her microphone.

"Eli, where's Smeared Lipstick? We need them onstage in twenty."

"They just got out of makeup. Heading over now."

"Great." She turned to Sara. "I need you to come with me. Jake asked for you."

Jake Prescott, as in her boss. As in, the guy who'd barely spoken two words to her since she'd been hired. What could he possibly want? A quick glance back at Daxton confirmed he'd settled back into his role, the mask firmly in place.

"Don't look so panicked." Casie winked. "It's not like he's going to fire you or anything."

Unless someone had witnessed her spewing insults at one of the hottest names in music, after assaulting him with her boobs. "If you say so." She'd like nothing more than to be sprawled over him again, wet, sticky, insanely aroused… Argh! What was wrong with her? Fantasizing about a guy she'd despised such a short time ago? Because they shared an unspoken moment that probably meant absolutely nothing?

Eli squeezed her shoulder. *"Counting the minutes."*

She managed a weak smile, her stomach in knots. "Can't wait." *Liar.*

Casie grabbed her wrist, yanking her toward the door. "Eli is so flipping hot. Do you know how many girls would drop their panties for him?"

"Yeah…" A heady scent filled her nostrils, intoxicating her senses, as Daxton strode past. She choked back a gasp, stumbling backward into a wall.

"Your boyfriend's a lucky guy," he murmured, his

half-hooded gaze yanking off every stitch of still-sticky clothing covering her overly sensitized body. Uttering a response was useless, since she'd pretty much been rendered mute, left to silently mull the wicked thoughts looping through her mind as she admired that perfect ass vacate the room.

Boyfriend? What boyfriend?

FOUR

"OKAY GUYS, WE'RE SWITCHING UP the public relations team for the rest of the tour." Merrick walked into the dimly lit green room at the arena and folded his arms. "Since Finn can't keep his dick in his pants, we need a new junior publicist on the road with us."

"Hey, how is this my fault? I happen to think she was real good at her job."

"Yeah, but it didn't include blowing you when she was supposed to be handling logistics for press conferences. Remember what happened with the sound system the first time you plugged her?" Cooper snickered into his beer, the mere sound making Daxton's shoulders tense. His fists clenched, primed to land a satisfying blow to the jaw, but pummeling Cooper now would only cause more headaches

27

later.

"Ah, yeah." Finn stretched his legs out on the plush rust colored sofa. "Damn straight, I do."

"Yeah, *somebody* didn't flip off her mike." Daxton rolled his eyes. "Can we at least get two this time? One as a back-up, you know, just in case?"

Finn winked at him. "Daxy knows the deal. At least one will fall prey to my boyish good looks and charm."

"Let's just say I think we should hedge our bets."

Merrick nodded. "I'm meeting with Jake Prescott from the record label tomorrow to finalize the details. The plan is to keep the senior publicity team, led by Asya, on the ground in Houston and take a junior rep on the road, who can handle the day to day bullshit. It'll be good. We'll still have Kat with us to handle all the social media."

"Oohh, I like the idea of a newbie. That'll be fun. They're always so star struck. It's like you're God, you know?" Finn smirked.

Liam let out a loud yawn. "I don't know. Lacie calls me God all the time. I don't need to be banging publicists to feed my ego."

"Whatever, dude. You're one half of a practically married couple on tour with some of the hottest chicks on the planet itching for a chance to get in your pants. Lacie's cool as shit, but you're wasting your youth. I mean, let's face it, you're not really that talented. Once the ladies find *that* out…" Finn snickered and punched Liam in the shoulder. "…you'll have missed your shot."

"Leave the guy alone. It's cute he wants to stay faithful to his high school sweetheart. Makes him more irresistible."

Merrick popped the cap off his beer bottle.

Cooper's blue-eyed gaze was unwavering, singularly focused on Daxton. Unspoken words hung between them in the form of accusations and harsh expletives, ones that would create a world of chaos if they ever tumbled forth. "Don't listen to those idiots. You're a lucky guy, Liam."

"Thanks, Coop. I know it." Liam took a large gulp of water. "Maybe someday you guys'll find the right ones, too. Until then, plug away. Just keep the presents wrapped, you know what I'm saying?"

Daxton clenched the bottle of scotch, envisioning Cooper's neck in his firm grasp. Rage bubbled beneath the surface, threatening to erupt through his pores until Cooper finally averted his eyes, studying his beer before taking a long swig. This bullshit façade…how much longer could Daxton bury his anger and disgust? Shielding it from the rest of the guys…the physical anguish of maintaining civility when what he really wanted to do was smash Cooper's fucking head into a cinderblock wall. Christ, an explosion was imminent, and he pitied anyone whose ass was close enough to get singed by the flames.

A knock sounded and Casie appeared in the doorway, iPad in hand, Bluetooth headset firmly in place. "You're on in five, guys. Let's move."

Fucking Cooper. So many unresolved and pent-up emotions coursed through Daxton's veins. As if he didn't have enough of his own crap anchoring him, now he had to deal with that whole mess.

He watched the guys shuffle out of the room, happy, settled, free from demons, able to enjoy the success they'd created together. But Daxton's memory was polluted with angst, resentment, and remorse, the effects of which could never be eradicated, no matter how much sex, booze, or any other mind-altering substance he could consume. This success, this *life*, was more like a nightmare on continuous loop, one where he was the one perpetually hunted with no refuge.

One person had seen what lurked beneath the layers - everything people expected from him, but nothing they really knew. Sara had witnessed what stewed in his soul and shredded his heart because he'd let her in for the briefest of moments during that press conference. He'd never exposed that part of himself to anyone. It was strangely arousing, as fucked up as that was to admit. But he'd done it because he sensed she'd understand, unlike everyone else in his life. Call it intuition, instinct, whatever the hell. It rarely failed him.

FIVE

JESUS, IF ELI'S TONGUE PLUNGED ANY further down her throat, it'd probably hit her intestines. Except Sara really wasn't in the mood to be swallowed whole. Not hot. Not seductive. Definitely not tonight, when she could think of little other than Daxton's penetrating eyes, so deep and dark, his low, husky voice, and those powerful fingers strumming a haunting melody for a stadium full of screaming fans entranced by his broodiness. Oh yeah, and the offer she'd received from the big boss, Jake Prescott.

Eager hands lifted the hem of her Green Lantern t-shirt, one of the first cool things she'd actually bought herself to replace the bland ones that had populated the otherwise stuffy wardrobe she'd carted from her home in Grand Falls, Minnesota. They were clothes for a different girl…from a very different time.

Cold fingertips traveled over her skin, persistent and demanding. Goose bumps popped up along her arms and they were not the ones of a delicious variety. This particular type warned of impending nausea, a sensation that did not evoke anything remotely resembling arousal.

Daxton, on the other hand, had fingers that could surely sizzle anything they grazed. But he was all wrong for her. If what she'd seen behind his gaze at the press conference was real, she'd fall right into his downward spiral because two lost souls couldn't possibly—

Boom. And there was reason number one why she couldn't take Jake up on his offer. A newbie getting the coveted chance to go on tour with Jimmy Sixx? An opportunity to learn the ropes and the business from the inside? Nothing less than a dream. But to be around rocker bad boy, Daxton Cole, pretty much twenty-four seven, a guy who had become a permanent fixture on her mind since her body had been plastered over his only hours earlier? It was a freaking disaster in the making. And if that weren't enough, toss in the part about her slightly territorial boyfriend Eli being picked to manage the opening band, Smeared Lipstick, on the *same* tour. Devastation of epic proportions.

She pulled away, breathless. "Stop."

"What's going on with you? You've been acting weird ever since we left the arena."

Her eyes scoured every inch of the carpet. *Needs a good vacuuming.* "I'm fine. Just tired. It was a long day."

"I thought we were celebrating tonight." He inched

closer, nuzzling her neck, making the little hairs stand on end. "You're not in the mood now?"

God, what an understatement. How could her feelings have shifted so abruptly? Not that she'd been ready to race down the aisle, but…Oh hell, she must be really sleep deprived. That had to be it. There was no other excuse for this ridiculous infatuation. She hadn't even known who Daxton was before this afternoon. "I just…I don't really feel…well." Not exactly a lie, since her gag reflex kicked in once Eli's abnormally long, serpent-like tongue collided with the back of her throat.

His fingertips drummed on the coffee table, the sound reverberating between her ears. When had it become so irritating? And that knee, could he keep it from bouncing for a mere five seconds?

"You just need to relax." His eyes glittered. "I can help with that. You look so hot right now. Is it so wrong to want…"

Blah, blah, blah. The words kept flowing, but she only saw his lips flapping. Good Lord, what was happening to her? All of a sudden, her feelings for Eli, albeit lukewarm, curdled like expired milk because her otherwise-lucid mind couldn't manage to rid itself from the captivating hold of one Daxton Cole, a rock star with a questionable past. She'd finally tapped those six little letters onto her iPhone keyboard and done some recon. Google rewarded her with a goldmine of information, as well as confirmation that said rocker was rowing a boatload of issues through hostile waters. Truth, fiction, nobody knew for sure, but everyone had judged. Hence, the problem with hearsay, something she knew all too well.

"You're tense. So tight. I can feel it." Eli's hands kneaded her shoulders, no doubt looking for any opportunity to slide under her shirt. "Wanna smoke? I got some killer weed from this guy."

"What! When did you start smoking?" A chill shimmied down Sara's spine, heart thrumming against her ribcage. Was she really that oblivious? How could she have missed his tell? Or maybe that was just the problem with burying your head in the sand for too long. After a while, you just blissfully suffocate in your own ignorance.

"That's very cute." He pulled out a dime bag and some rolling papers. "Just wait. A few pulls of this and all that tension will disappear. It's like magic. And the sex will be awesome."

She wrung her hands together. "Eli, please, I'm just not—"

"Not what? I don't recall you complaining when I had you coming six ways to Sunday the other night."

Yeah, about that… Whatever, it'd be her little secret.

He sprinkled out the contents remaining in the bag, rolled, and sealed it. Sara's stomach flipped as she watched him. Panic rose in her throat, her body already feeling the effects of what her mind buried long ago. *Stop him! Don't let him do it!* Eli grabbed a lighter and with a flick of his thumb, he inhaled deeply as the end ignited.

The pungent odor assaulted her nostrils, inciting her senses, until the memories plaguing her subconscious sprung to life. How quickly the fear had returned, along with the knowledge that she could run until her legs could no longer carry her. But in the end, evil never would perish. The text she'd received was proof positive of that.

SIX

DAXTON HAD BEEN STRUMMING THE strings of his guitar for hours on end, but words refused to come. Nothing fit, nothing was right. Not in his heart or head, not since the night Sara Russell had barreled into his already-complicated-enough life with her jackass boyfriend in tow. It had been a couple of days since the last show in Houston. The tour was on a brief hiatus, and her absence only threw his mind into overdrive. A much needed break from the craziness of the tour had turned out to be the exact opposite of relaxing, despite the blowjobs, three-ways, and excess of booze filling his days. If anything, it all amplified the void, knowing what he craved was just beyond reach. And he needed to eradicate that craving, since it was a guaranteed dead-end. He had so little to offer; after years of being stripped of all self-worth by his father, he never felt like he truly belonged, like he'd ever really mattered, especially in comparison to Jase. Hell, if his own mother could just pick up and—

A loud knock sent him jumping into the air. That always seemed to happen when he was deep in the abyss of his troubled thoughts. He looked up to see Merrick lounging in the doorway of the studio.

"You scared the shit out of me. What the hell is up, Cue Ball?"

"That's a new one. Always quick with the nicknames. Too bad you can't come up with lyrics at that speed." Merrick smirked and flopped into a chair. "I figured I'd find you here. Trying to stay sober long enough to make that solo album you keep hinting about? Kudos, man."

"Staying sober isn't the problem. You know I do my best writing after I've knocked back a few."

"Yeah, a few *dozen*."

"What can I say? I have a lot of angst."

"I know you *give* people a lot of angst. Like yours truly. You're lucky I haven't drop-kicked your ass after all these years."

Daxton slid his guitar into its case and stood, stretching his arms overhead. "I give as good as I get."

"I'll take your word on that one. So, let's talk about the next album. The label is on my ass non-stop for release dates."

"I thought we could at least finish the tour before committing to anything."

"Dax, you're the front man for this band. The guys look to you for leadership. I know things have been tough, but

37

you need to make a call. You're dragging your feet, and it's impacting a hell of a lot of people."

Why couldn't a long gulp of water just wash away all the anger that plagued him? It satiated his thirst, but that was all. It was too innocuous, too pure to battle so much darkness, unlike his pals Jack, Jim, and Johnny. They made everything brighter, albeit temporarily. But he couldn't expect Merrick to understand. Nobody did. And damn, it was hard to find his way through the murk when he'd never been able to see the light.

Merrick cocked an eyebrow. "And let's face it, you're too much of a moody bitch to find another manager who'd be able to stand you for longer than a day. If you keep dicking around, you'll be washed up at the age of twenty-four. Even best friends have limits."

"I know you'd never let that happen, Q-Bert. We've been through too much together."

"Yeah…" Gone was the sarcastic tone, the playful expression now eclipsed by something much more serious, deep…puzzling? Unsettling was a definite candidate. Somehow, the spirited mood had taken a nosedive into hair-raising. It was an odd intensity; one he'd never witnessed before from Merrick, and never cared to again.

Merrick opened his mouth after a drawn-out moment of borderline uncomfortable silence, but still no words emerged.

Daxton furrowed his brow. "Dude, did you just black out or something? Looks like you're in a trance. What gives?"

Merrick's signature ringtone blared from his pocket. He

raked a hand through his hair, averting his eyes. "Quinn."

After guzzling the rest of the water, Daxton picked up his guitar. The stress and pressure of this life – Jesus, it slammed everyone into the ground.

"No fucking way. How?"

The strings vibrated against his fingers, his mind conjuring up a certain sultry green-eyed gaze. Forget everything he'd never be; he knew what he'd be capable of being if Sara gave him a chance. He plucked the chords, half-fantasizing about Sara's lush breasts in his face. A replay of that might bust him out of his writing funk. They'd been so close to his mouth, beckoning him, begging for a quick nip.

"Jesus Christ, do you remember that chick you banged before the show the other night? The backup singer for Smeared Lipstick? Brandi?" Merrick clicked off his phone, back in action. Whatever had commanded him only moments earlier had dissipated. Good thing, since Daxton had no idea how to relate to grim and sinister Merrick. He much preferred the lewd and obnoxious persona.

Brandi. That was her name. "I didn't bang her, but yeah, vaguely. I remember some of the choice words she used after I kicked her out of my dressing room."

"What do you mean, you didn't bang her?" A look of shock flitted across Merrick's face.

"I mean we didn't fuck, moron. But the more pressing question is, why do you care?"

Merrick let out a snort. "As if I need to live vicariously through you, dickhead. That was Casie. There was some kind of accident. The girl wrapped her car around a tree."

"Holy shit, are you serious? Is she going to be okay?"

"Casie said her hip's busted up and her leg's broken in about a billion places. Messed up, right?"

"Damn." He slid the guitar pick between his fingers. "Maybe I should have banged her after all. Kinda like a last hurrah since it seems like she'll be out of commission for a while."

I T WAS HARD NOT TO BE STAR STRUCK AS she literally brushed elbows with some of the top names in music. Studio 713 in Houston was a hotbed for A-list recording artists. Sara stole a quick look at her watch. Ten minutes to spare. Casie's instructions had been very clear: Noon meeting with Merrick Quinn, Studio A. There was no way she'd risk blowing another assignment, especially when the need to get the hell out of dodge was suddenly immediate and necessary.

Daxton Cole's best friend and manager had the reputation for being a certifiable prick, but his hands were tied. The record label mandated that the bad boy rocker either clean up his act or hire someone to magically erase the seemingly endless indiscretions. A shiver slithered down her spine at the irony. Play with fire, it was almost a guarantee you'd get burned. That text was all the proof she'd needed. It had been so out of the blue, appearing on her phone just after she'd accepted Jake's offer to join the tour. Someone knew…but who?

You'll never outrun the truth, Sara. And you'll pay for your sins.

Thinking she'd be able to escape the past…how ridiculous. The truth would always surface. But she needed this job, so she'd do anything to convince them otherwise.

Sara wandered the halls, searching for Studio A, nibbling her already bitten down fingernails. Thankfully, this place was way smaller than the City Center Arena, so she might even arrive earlier than planned. Wouldn't that be miraculous? Punctuality had never been her forte. She frowned at her reflection in a wall of mirrored plaques. All the makeup and trendy clothes in Texas could never disguise the ugliness that lurked in her soul. On the outside, her look was a perfect fit for this lifestyle, but underneath it all, fear, remorse, and regret blurred the designer labels. A quick yank of her skirt took it from obscene to borderline inappropriate, but the shirt was too tight to adjust. The rumbling in her belly became more persistent, though food was the last thing on Sara's mind. How much longer could she hide behind this new image? How many more lies would she have to tell before someone saw through her? A little bit of reconnaissance would easily reveal information her parents had been so intent to bury.

Heated voices from inside Studio A stopped her mid-knock. The door was slightly ajar. Crap. It was almost time. She chewed the inside of her glossed lip, eyes darting up and down the desolate hallway. Should she go inside? What if Merrick was in there? Argh! Was it better to be late or nosy?

"Don't ever tell me I have to do *anything*, Cooper. If you had any shred of decency or intelligence, you'd be thinking long and hard before directing me."

The voice sounded familiar, but it was too low to confirm. Whoever it was, he sure had some beef with a guy named Cooper. The hair on Sara's arms stood at attention. Cooper. Jimmy Sixx. Jeez, when the heck was she going to get it together? She could have at least remembered their names, for the love of Pete. Or maybe the very real threat of being stalked had her slightly preoccupied.

"Listen, I know you're still angry, but it's not up to you to decide the fate of the band."

A low, hollow laugh emerged from the studio. "Are you really going to blame this on me after you fucking destroyed everything?"

"Dax, I—"

"I don't give a fuck what you have to say anymore. Do you understand? It's over. Just be thankful I haven't replaced your scumbag ass already. But make no mistake, you're the fuck *out*."

Jesus Christmas. Daxton Cole was in there, and it sounded like he might be on the verge of a killing spree, not about to finish the final leg of their sold-out platinum tour.

"Sara Russell?"

She swallowed a yelp and spun in the direction of the approaching voice. The Bluetooth earpiece gave away his identity in an instant. The blue-tipped spiky black hair was a close second clue.

"Um, yes. Merrick, right?" With a forced smile, she walked toward him.

A slow grin spread over his face. Tall, built, trendy – everything you'd expect from the manager of a handful of rock gods. The blue hair complimented his cobalt eyes; cold, as they were critical. He didn't even try to hide it as he sized her up, strip-searching her from top to bottom. Blech. Talk about feeling violated, and he hadn't even shaken her hand. *Jerk.*

"Come on in so we can discuss the details." Merrick brushed past her, pulling open the door. "I want you to meet…Coop, what are you doing here?"

Cooper's face flushed an alarming shade of purple. "Hey, I was, ah, just going." He grabbed his jacket and left without so much as a backward glance.

Daxton toyed with a guitar pick, the heat of his gaze darn near melting the skin off her bones. *What is it with this guy?* How could he be so sexy one minute, singeing her insides with a sweep of those deliciously dark eyes and spew venom like a viper the next? Maybe the more apt question was, why was she so aroused by the metamorphosis? "Been here long?"

A sharp gasp escaped her lips. Shoot, she'd been caught. "Uh, no, I um… just met Merrick outside and we uh—"

"Good. Hate to scare you off before you're even offered the job." He pointed to Merrick. "Q, what do you think?"

Merrick's leer, which was more of an assault than a mere look, made her knees lock. Did she really want to be on the road with that sleaze, *if* she got the job? Scratch that.

She needed this position. It was the rapid exit into oblivion, something she'd been desperate for the second that airplane took off from Grand Falls.

"I think she looks good. Real good. Lots of potential." Another once-over made her skin crawl. *Eww.*

"You're going to scare her off."

As if.

"I think it would be a great opportunity, since I'm new to all this. I have a fresh perspective and a lot of ideas about how we can polish up your image – through charities, goodwill, interviews. Rest assured, I'll work tirelessly to make sure you're fully satisfied with the results." What a joke. If she couldn't fix her own mess, how the heck was she going to fix Daxton Cole's?

"*Nice.* So, tirelessly, does that mean all day, all night, until he's done… working?" Ick. Could Merrick be any slimier? The salad she'd scarfed down less than an hour ago was ready to project vomit all over the soundboards.

A snicker slipped from Merrick's lips. "Okay, I'm done messing with you. But you need thick skin if you're gonna hang with these guys, especially this one. The press has been relentless, and it's only going to get worse. You've got your work cut out for you. I just wanted to see how much you could handle."

"Before you made me vomit all over my boots?"

"Basically." Merrick grinned. "She's in. I'll let Jake know we'll take the newbie."

"Gee, thanks for the endorsement." The sly quip fell from her mouth, but she didn't bother to yank it back. Enough with the shrinking violet crap. This was her new chapter. Heck, it was a brand-new novel, and she was penning the scenes.

"Okay, we're done here. Sara, I'll have Jake send you the logistics about the tour dates and—"

"Wait." Dax stopped plucking the strings of his guitar. Jeez, why couldn't she tear her eyes from his long, powerful fingers stemming from those large palms? Holy cow, the things he could probably do with those hands...

"What?" Merrick furrowed his brow.

"Not you, her." The strumming began once again, the melody making her body hum right along with the instrument.

Merrick's eyes narrowed to slits, chilling her from the tips of her toes to her now-clammy fingertips. "What about *her*?"

"Don't I get a crack at her before we finalize anything?"

"You've never asked permission before."

"I'm not starting now. It was a rhetorical question." Dax snickered. He patted the empty stool next to him. "Have a seat. *Newbie.*"

Merrick raked a hand through his tousled hair. "Keep it short. Too much time with you, and she'll probably go running back to Bumble Fuck, North Dakota or wherever the hell she's from."

"Minnesota." She cocked an eyebrow. "I didn't realize you had such animosity toward the Midwest."

"Some things just have a funny way of setting me off." The caustic words were directed at her, but his eyes were glued to Daxton's face. Jeez, what the heck was eating this guy? As if he'd never witnessed a purging of sexual innuendoes. Lord knew Merrick had probably experienced a heck of a lot more than just words being tossed around. Maybe he wanted in, until Daxton unceremoniously tossed him out.

And guys thought women were hard to read?

Daxton's rumpled white shirt fell slightly open, exposing his tanned, taut chest. God, did she want to run her tongue over the grooves of his abs.

"Tell me about yourself."

"I, um…relocated here from Grand Falls, Minnesota. I've always wanted to get into the entertainment industry." Her eyes fell to his feet. Black Under Armour sneakers sat on the floor next to his stool, his toes wiggling in a pair of mismatched socks. *Hmm…laundry day?*

"Pretty sweet gig for someone so green."

Was there a hint of disbelief in that statement? "My parents had a few connections."

"Nice they wanted to look out for you."

"Yeah…" The urge to chomp her nails was so darned strong. To keep some degree of control when the rest of her existence spiraled into a million different directions just beyond her reach. His persistent gaze held so many questions; ones she wasn't willing to answer; ones she didn't want to acknowledge.

"You're a tough read. Let's try something simpler. What's your favorite food?"

"Grape popsicles." No hesitation there, not when it came to her one vice. Until that moment, she hadn't figured out how to indulge her taste buds in the one pleasure she'd allowed herself since fleeing Minnesota. Did those tour buses have freezers? It wasn't like there was a green room request contract for the junior publicist. She'd have to settle for grape-flavored gum or lollipops. Not horrible alternatives.

"Cold, grape-flavored tongue…lots of interesting possibilities," he mused, eyes on the guitar he was strumming.

Her fingers twitched. She slammed her hands between her knees. Not biting, not biting. "Just so I'm clear, is the innuendo part of the interview? Or just out there for your own personal enjoyment?"

"Thick skin, remember?" He snickered. "So, you're a professional fixer. Ever find anyone worth saving?"

"Aren't we all worthy of redemption?"

Daxton shrugged. "Some more than others."

She swallowed hard, only to find a lump in her throat, barely able to choke out the words. "Everyone deserves a chance to atone. Don't you know there are always three sides to every story?"

"In my case, they're all the same."

"Don't you think it's important to change that perception? Wouldn't your brother have wanted that for you?"

His dark eyes flashed. "You don't know anything about me. Don't pretend to think you do just because you read something about my dead brother."

Perspiration drizzled down her spine. "Oh my gosh, I didn't mean to…I just, um…I'm so sorry."

He let out a groan. "Fuck. I shouldn't have snapped like that. It's not you, okay? It's everybody else. Nobody gives a damn about what I'm going through. All they care about is keeping their cash cow from going down in flames. Am I upset? Yes. Am I fucked in the head? Not entirely. I'm *grieving*. So what if I do it with a bottle of Jack and a threesome on occasion?"

Who the hell was she to tell this guy how to live his life when her own was such a mess? She had more skeletons than closets, for heaven's sake. And forget that she'd like to be part of said threesome. "You know what? You're right. If that's what you need, so be it. Grieve, Daxton. Let it all go. I've got your back, and I'll be there to collect all the cell phones so nobody can exploit it on YouTube."

"Sounds like you're in. I'm not too much of a train wreck for you?"

His grin had her insides twisted like pretzels. "Self-awareness is the first step. We just need to capitalize on your endearing qualities."

"You're assuming I have them." The words sounded so flip, a stark contrast to the sadness lurking in his gaze.

"No, I'm inferring. I never assume." The corners of her lips curled into a smile. "And if you don't have them, I'll just make something up. I'm a publicist, not an investigative reporter for CNN. It's all in the spin."

D AXTON LISTENED TO SARA'S FINGERS fly over the keyboard of her MacBook Air at breakneck speed. He was more of a hunt and peck kind of guy, but hell, he'd rather be masterful with other things finger-related. Her eyes narrowed at the laptop screen, lips pursed. It wouldn't have been a shock to see smoke billowing from her ears at any second.

He stared at the Snow White decal on the laptop lid. Just like Sara, she was innocent and naïve. Of course, that's where the similarity ended. Snow White would have been appalled at Sara's skimpy wardrobe choices and probably wouldn't have known how to formulate a snarky comment, much less utter one. Quite the dichotomy between perception and reality.

"Ever worry about carpal tunnel syndrome?"

She cracked a half-smile, still typing. "My fingers are pretty agile."

"I think that comment requires some kind of validation. If you need some suggestions, I'd be happy to—"

Her green eyes floated up from the screen. "I'm sure you would. But that's not why I'm here today."

He sighed and sank into the soft corduroy recliner in his massive living room. It was cream-colored, definitely not something he'd ever select. But his decorator insisted it worked like a charm in the expansive space. Earth-tones and airy accents. Whatever the hell. "Right. Today we commence Operation Reboot Daxton Cole."

"You're not that hopeless." *Click, click, click.*

"I might believe that if you volunteered any bit of the insight you've already shared with that laptop."

Sara closed the lid and drummed her alleged agile fingers on the coffee table. Damn, it was hard not to look... and wonder. "I'm working on an idea for a charity event for you and the guys. I've done some research, and I like the idea of doing some kind of concert to benefit disease research, like cancer. It's something you've been close to and I—"

"No."

A look of confusion flitted over her features. "What do you mean, 'no'?"

"If I want to donate my time or money to help sick kids, I do it. I won't exploit them to rehabilitate my tarnished image." He gritted his teeth. "I'm not on board with that."

"It's not exploiting anyone. It's raising awareness of a need for medical research, resources, or any help for a cure.

Donations can help families who can't afford medical care for their kids. The money can give them a fighting chance. How can you be opposed to helping, especially after..." She paused, biting her lower lip. "...after what happened to your brother? These kids are all someone's brother, sister, son, or daughter. I don't understand why you're so closed off to the idea."

"Look, Sara. I can appreciate your position, but I've made my own bed, along with a hell of a lot of suck-ass choices. I have to live with my situation. I'll temper my actions, but I won't beg for mercy. I'm not a bad person, and I'm definitely not a phony driven by image."

"That's a very nice speech, but you *are* accountable - to yourself, to the band, to the label, and to your fans. This can be a quick fix."

He snickered. *Oh, the naiveté.* All the snark in the universe couldn't erase it. "Come on, sweetheart. There's no quick fix for anything about me. I'm complex, tormented, soulless...haven't you read the papers?"

"That's not who you really are." She leaned in, a strand of blonde hair falling over her right eye. He longed to brush it back, to tuck it into place, and then run his hands through the rest of it, pulling her closer, tasting those pouty pink lips.

"You sound pretty sure about that. How can everyone else be wrong?"

"They don't see what I see."

"And what do you see? Humor me." He toyed with the cardboard wrapped around his Starbucks coffee cup.

A soft smile tugged those sinful lips upward. "I see

someone who's acting out because he doesn't know how to accept his circumstances."

"What if I don't want to accept them?"

"Then figure out how to change them."

"Ever hear of lost causes?"

"I'm not saying everything in your life can be repaired with the flick of a switch. But if you accept your situation and try to make positive changes, that's progress. Things may not be perfect, but you'll be true to yourself, and forgive me for saying so, but I'm pretty sure you're hiding behind those vices because it's safer than baring your soul and being perceived as vulnerable."

"I thought you were a publicist, not a shrink."

She winked. "Double major in college."

"I'm still not doing any of it."

"Okay. It was only one of my ideas and I wouldn't be a very good publicist if I didn't have an arsenal of other press-battling weapons." She re-opened the lid of her laptop.

"Your fingers haven't cramped up yet?"

"Nope."

Click, click, click. The speed was impressive. And her ten-cent therapy session wasn't too far off base. "I guess I'll just wait until your fingers need another break before you divulge the next—" His iPhone vibrated on the table, the number on the screen stopping him mid-sentence. He jumped up and stabbed the Accept button. "Hey, Millie."

Sara's eyes crept upward, though her fingers never stopped moving. Avoiding her gaze, he walked toward the large picture window, watching the crystal blue waters of the waterfall spilling into his Olympic-sized swimming pool. "How's Luke doing?"

Millie, the head nurse at the Children's Cancer Center at MD Anderson, let out a deep sigh. "Not good, Dax. He really wants to see you. I know you're busy, but things aren't looking good."

The tightness in Daxton's chest squeezed the oxygen from his lungs. He wanted to cry, to throw things, to scream for the mercy of this little boy, who wouldn't have a chance to live much beyond his nine years. They'd become fast friends ever since Luke had become Jase's roommate. After Jase passed away, Daxton continued to visit Luke and the other kids whenever he had down time, even though it hurt like hell not to see his brother in the crowd of smiling faces. He wrote new songs for the kids, brought treats, and gave music lessons… anything to make them happy and hopeful, since there was so much darkness clouding their days.

"I'll be there in half an hour."

"Thanks, Dax. It'll mean so much to him." Relief was evident in Millie's voice. The sharp pang in his chest warned him that he was on borrowed time. His friend needed him.

"I'll see you soon." Daxton clicked off the phone and squeezed his eyes shut to keep the tears from falling. Things were always going to end in this way, but dammit, he wasn't prepared. It was too much of a harsh reminder of Jase's final days. How quickly the Band-Aids had been ripped from wounds that were now open, raw, and exposed. Memories exploded in his mind…Jase's cold, lifeless fingers laced with his own, his pale face and vacant expression, his withered body against the stark white sheets.

Pull it together. Be there for someone else. Do it for Luke. Do it for Jase. Do it for yourself.

"Daxton?"

He raked a hand through his hair, still staring out the window. "I have to go."

"We only have a few more days before the tour starts up again. There's a lot more to cover."

"It can wait. This can't."

"Um, okay. Can I come with you? Maybe we can keep talking for a while longer? I have a meeting with Jake tomorrow, and he's going to want—"

"I don't give a flying fuck about Jake. And no, you can't come. I have to do this alone."

Her scent wafted in the air around him. Something tropical, maybe coconut. It reminded him of his mother's favorite lotion. The one she'd taken away forever, along with everything else. His stomach twisted.

"Hey, I don't know who was on the phone, but you don't have to push me away. I want to help." Her hand grazed his arm. Warmth flooded him, bringing comfort and protection from the ensuing pain. "Let me be there for you, Daxton. The weight of the world doesn't need to rest on your shoulders alone."

He turned, meeting her questioning gaze. Her mere presence was so strong; his body couldn't help gravitating toward it. There were so many conflicting emotions in her expression – confusion, worry, sadness, and hope. She trusted without evidence, had faith with no rationale. Why did she think he was worthy of her time and concern? His actions did nothing to convince her otherwise, but yet, here she was, offering herself, and looking for nothing in return. So unlike everyone else on this goddamned planet.

"Okay," he whispered. "But this isn't for the press. This is just for you, understand?"

Sara gripped the leather bucket seat, hoping the queasy sensation in her belly would finally settle. For the past twenty minutes, Daxton swerved his midnight blue Ferrari in and out of lanes on the freeway, en route to some unknown destination. He hadn't divulged anything during the ride, and she'd spent the better part of that time biting off her nail polish, and the rest of the time praying for her life.

She let out a shuddering breath when a large set of mirrored glass buildings came into view. The Houston Medical Center? Did this visit have something to do with his brother? What was so time-sensitive that it couldn't wait until the following day?

With one final maneuver, the car came to a screeching halt, right in front of the MD Anderson Cancer Center. The setting sun glowed over the pavilion glittering on the reflective windows. The buildings sat in the midst of a lush landscape of brightly colored flowers and shrubbery. But what would greet them beyond the entrance?

"Sara."

"Yes?" Her voice was so soft, almost inaudible to herself.

"I'm sorry for dragging you with me. I should have told you the circumstances, but I..." He let out a deep sigh. "...I guess I liked the idea of not being alone after all."

"Alone for what?" She fought the temptation to gnaw the loose cuticle on her thumb. "I'm here for you. You can tell me."

"There's a little guy in there who's in bad shape. My friend. His name is Luke. After Jase passed away, I kept coming to visit and help out with the kids. Luke and I became buddies. But he's really sick, and they don't know how much longer..." His eyes drifted to the building in front of them. "I need to be here for him."

She reached over and squeezed his hand, startled when he squeezed it back. Holy cow, did she not even realize what she'd done? "Let's go see your friend."

They walked into the main building, passing the large, wood-paneled reception area. Daxton had a smile for everyone he passed. Gone was the brooding, tortured soul the tabloids spoke of; the guy the rest of the world *thought* they knew vanished. He stooped to give high-fives to the younger kids and cracked corny jokes for the older ones. And darn it, if he wasn't just like the Pied Piper, collecting more and more kids as they made their way through mosaic-painted corridors toward Luke's wing.

A heavy-set nurse with kind eyes and a warm, welcoming smile greeted them when they entered. "It's so good to see you, sweetie." She pulled Daxton into her arms, gaze set on Sara. "Who's this young lady? A *fan*?"

He snickered. "Hardly. She's my new publicist. Sara, say hi to Millie. She's the backbone of this whole facility."

"Hi, it's really nice to meet you." It was hard not to smile. Millie was a ray of sunshine, exactly what these kids needed on a daily basis.

"Likewise." Millie grinned and nodded toward Daxton. "So, you've got your work cut out for you with this one, huh?"

Sara giggled. "You know it."

"Dax, are you gonna sing for us tonight?" One of the little girls tugged his black leather jacket.

He bent down and ruffled her long blonde ringlets. "Maybe a little later if it's not too late. I need to go see Luke first, okay, Carly?"

Carly beamed and she threw her arms around his neck. "Okay!"

An excited squeal pierced the air as Daxton swung Carly around before setting her back on the floor. "Keep an eye on these guys for me in the meantime."

Carly gave him the thumbs-up and snuggled into Millie. "You've got it, Dax!" It was quite possibly one of the most adorable things Sara had ever seen.

He laced his fingers with Sara's. "Come on. We'll be back later."

Sara's sneakers squeaked on the polished tile floor, the only sound her body was capable of making since her brain and her mouth were suddenly at odds and simultaneously on strike. It was like all of the happiness in Daxton's world resided here in this cluster of buildings, a place where every second, every smile, every encounter was treasured, because in a blink, it could all be gone. Forever. A cold and senseless reality lurked beyond the vibrant colors and cheerful décor.

"Why do you give in to the grief, Daxton?" She tugged

on his hand, unable to take another step until she'd spoken the words, the lump in her throat all but suffocating her. "Why do you let it consume you? The drinking, the women, the drugs…how can that provide you any comfort? This whole place…" She waved her arms around the empty corridor. "…the kids, the staff…they love you. You bring them happiness and comfort. How could you not focus on all of the good you can do for others? I'm sorry if that's out of line, but—"

He dropped her hand and collapsed against a wall that was full of brightly colored yellow sunflowers. "Sara, do you realize this is the one place where I can be myself? Where I'm actually happy, because I know, for even a little while, I can make the kids forget about the horrors that haunt them every day?"

"But then why do you—"

"I can't be here all the time. Shit happens when I'm gone and it's bad. Sometimes it's easier to drown my thoughts instead of letting them eat me alive. For a little while, it doesn't hurt as much when the phone calls come, and I hear I've lost another one of my friends. That I didn't get a chance to say goodbye."

Tears pooled in her eyes. God, watching him, hearing the pain in his voice…it felt like her heart was breaking in two. A slow, agonizing pain seeped into her chest. "Daxton, I'm so sorry. I didn't mean to upset you. I didn't…I didn't know."

He rested his head against the wall, a sad smile lifting his lips. "That's why we're here. Because my buddy, Luke, needs me."

Her heart thrummed with each step closer to Luke's room. She was afraid it might burst by the time they made it inside. Prayers were on constant loop in her mind. *Please let him be okay, please let him be pain-free, please let him be alive.*

"Dax!" A young boy with thinning blond hair was propped against a pile of pillows. An iPad sat on the table in front of him; some game with lots of characters shouting was open on the screen. A tired smile lit up his pale face. "You came."

"Of course I did. How could I not come to see my best pal?"

"But what about the tour?" Luke's voice was faint, tired, and breathless. Sara looked around the room. It was blue with soft yellow accents. No wires or machines lined the room. Just a bed, a laptop, lots of stuffed animals, and some super hero costumes. And Pez candy. Lots and lots of Pez.

"I have a little time before we start up again." Daxton pulled out an Iron Man Pez dispenser from the inside pocket of his jacket. "Here you go, bud."

When had he grabbed that? How had she missed it?

Luke turned his head toward Sara. "Who's that? She a groupie?"

Daxton chuckled. "Dude, you're nine. What do you know about groupies?"

"That's all you can say? Don't correct him or anything." Sara rolled her eyes. "I'm Sara, his publicist. My job is to make sure everyone thinks he's a good guy."

Luke's brow furrowed. "But he's already a good guy. So what do you get paid for?"

"Smart kid." Daxton pulled out a Nintendo DS game case and tossed it on the table. Santa Claus had nothing on this guy.

"Wow, Super Mario 3D World! Thanks, Dax!"

"Come on, let's play. I'll let you beat me."

Luke laughed. "You wish. I'm gonna wipe the floor with you."

Daxton poured some Gatorade into a cup and handed it to Luke. "You're gonna need the energy to keep up with my lightning fast hand-eye coordination."

"If you play video games the way you type on your phone, I think I'll be just fine."

"Ouch. That hurts, Luke." Daxton clutched his heart. "I came all the way here so you could make fun of me?"

"I'm your friend. And I've seen you take twenty minutes to type a password into my iPad. Don't you want me to be honest with you? Or does the truth hurt?"

"Dude! I'm insecure enough without you beating me into the ground."

Good God, this guy was making her melt faster than a box of chocolates sitting in the summer sun. Luke was animated, energized, and laughing, all because of Daxton. She pulled out her phone and snapped a couple of pictures to capture the pure joy on their faces. It was heartwarming... and heartbreaking at the same time.

"Do you want a turn?" Daxton flashed his famous grin at Sara. "Are you feeling brave?"

Sara laughed. "Nah, I'd prefer to watch you get your butt whipped by Luke."

"No faith. Ever think I'm letting him beat me?"

"Nope. I think you're in over your head." She cocked an eyebrow. "Am I right or am I right, Luke?"

Luke's mouth was too full of Pez candies to answer, but the rapid head bob confirmed his agreement. "Mmm-hmm!"

"I play to win. I don't like to lose." A flash of carnal hunger replaced the playfulness in Daxton's gaze and it chipped away at her resolve. No, no, no… she couldn't fall to pieces because of some semi-harmless suggestive language. *Hold it together. Let him know you're not giving away your hand.*

"Then start picking different opponents." There. She maintained control. Good. She could crumble later – still wondering, still lusting, but also still whole. His words spoke volumes: play to win. Well, she wasn't some damned trophy. Not for anyone. Not anymore.

A few games later, Luke was crowned the ruler of the Mushroom Kingdom. His eyes grew heavier and heavier with each passing game, but man, the little guy was a trooper. After their last bout, he let out a loud yawn and settled into the pillows. "Thanks so much for the game, Dax. I'm really glad you came."

Daxton gave him a fist bump. "You're the best, man. If you need anything, you call me, understand? I'll be back. I promise."

Luke nodded. "Okay," he whispered, his eyes fluttering closed.

She backed out of the room, leaving Daxton alone to watch Luke for a few moments. Her presence had already been enough of an intrusion to their guys' night activities. Would this be the last time Daxton saw Luke alive? It was a horrible question to acknowledge, but one that couldn't be avoided under the circumstances.

Moments later, Daxton walked out of the room. His face was tired, drawn, and concern etched his features. "Thanks for being here."

"Are you okay?"

He let out a deep sigh and leaned against the wall. It was almost as if his body had resigned itself to the fact that it couldn't rewrite the outcome of this chapter. "No. Definitely not okay."

"Daxton Cole. I heard you might be stopping by." A low male voice from behind made Sara jump. An adult version of Luke joined them outside the room. Handsome man, blond hair, bright smile. But his eyes were troubled, exhausted, and sad…so very sad.

"Keith, it's good to see you. This is my friend, Sara."

"Hi." A single pathetic word was all she could seem to utter, but what the heck else could she say? This man's son was living out his final days. All she wanted to do was crawl into a ball and weep for Luke and his family, for the life Luke would never get to experience, for the sorrows his survivors would carry forever.

"Thanks so much for coming. It means so much to him."

"Luke just fell asleep after a monster round of Super Mario. I also brought him some more Pez. You know they're like his super hero vitamins."

Keith smiled. "You've been a great friend to him, Dax. We appreciate everything you've done."

Daxton clapped him on the back. "Call me if you need

anything. Whenever, okay? I promise to get here as quickly as I can."

Keith nodded. "I will. Thank you both for being here." He walked into the room with a final wave.

They wandered back to the nurse's area. It was quiet. None of the kids were in sight. "Bedtime." Millie winked from behind the desk. "They need their rest so they can tear things up in the morning."

Sara smiled. Thank goodness these kids had someone like Millie watching over them. She was like their guardian angel on earth. "The kids are so lucky to have you."

"That's very sweet. I hope we'll see you again." Millie gave her a quick hug, pausing to whisper, "Dax is a very special guy. Please take care of him, honey."

A sob rose in her chest, and it took everything she had to fight it from erupting. "I will."

Daxton hugged Millie. "Tell Carly I promise I'll play for her next time."

"I will. Be safe, kids."

Silence descended as they walked to the parking lot. Sara pulled her denim jacket tight around her, shivering in the cool, crisp evening air.

"Cold?" He slung an arm around her, pulling her close. His normal musky scent had been replaced by something different...more fresh and clean. Soapy. Delicious. Delectable enough to—oh, for Pete's sake! It was amazing how just breathing him in could make her lose track of her sensibilities in a hot second.

He opened the car door for her and she slid into the seat. There was so much that she wanted to say, but nothing that could bring him peace. Ironic that they had similar demons to battle – both so tortured by what they couldn't change, both running from any degree of vulnerability because the risks were potentially too painful to accept. She nibbled on her thumbnail. The guy was unattainable, and she wasn't in the market to be acquired anyway, so why was her pulse racing like a car doing laps in the Indy 500?

"Hungry?"

His gravelly voice sliced through her thoughts. "Not really."

"Feasting on your nails is better than a real meal?"

"It's a bad habit, I know."

"So why do it? Do you know how bad it is to swallow all that nail polish?"

"It's kind of a control thing." She bit the inside of her lip and peered out the window at the cars whizzing past.

"How so?"

She let out a lingering breath. "Back in Grand Falls, I didn't have the best relationship with my parents. They're all about image. I always had to look a certain way, act a certain way, and wear my hair a certain way. It was maddening. My mom hated when I'd destroy a manicure before an event. So I kept doing it. It made me feel like I still had some control over myself." She twisted her hands. "That probably sounds stupid, huh?"

"No. I think we deal with our parents the best way we can. It's not always ideal, but if it helps us keep our sanity, so be it."

"Did your parents visit the facility as much as you?"

"Yeah."

"What about now?"

"My dad is more concerned with resurrecting his career than anything else. And my mom took off after Jase died. I haven't heard from her in a year."

"Daxton, I'm so sorry."

He shrugged. "It is what it is."

The remaining minutes of the ride back to Daxton's house were silent and thick with remorse. What kind of comforting words could she possibly offer when so many of her own unresolved issues shadowed her existence like a black cloud?

He pulled up next to her car and turned off the engine. "Do you want to come inside?"

Her chest tightened. "It's late. I think I should go."

"Are you sure?" Even a lack of light couldn't disguise the need in his eyes, but there was her screwed up life to consider, as well as the tour…and Eli. Besides, her new image didn't change who she really was on the inside, and that girl wanted much more than what Daxton was capable of giving.

She opened the door. "I'll put my notes together and see you in a few days. We'll talk then." Within seconds, she was in her own car, chewing on her nails once again. His hold on her was too strong, and if left to succumb to her feelings, she might very well choke.

NINE

S ARA CLUTCHED HER FLIMSY BLACK SHRUG tightly around her as she watched the roadies piling equipment to load onto the tour buses. It was expensive as all hell and barely covered any exposed skin. She doubted a giant fleece pullover would have warmed her at that point, since it wasn't the chill in the air frosting her insides. That moment in Daxton's car, the moonlight casting a glow over his lust-filled expression when he'd asked her to stay, was on permanent loop in her mind, much like the fantasies bridging the gap until she'd see him again, which was imminent.

Her jaw had dropped to the pavement when she saw the set of insanely huge buses they'd be boarding in a few short moments. Five-star luxury hotels on wheels, en route to Dallas, equipped with Lord only knew what to satisfy each band member's wanton desires. And would she ever like to satisfy Daxton Cole.

Oh crap. Was it really that impossible to conjure a single thought that didn't involve her lapping him up like a dog at a water bowl on a hot summer day? Way too much tingling going on in areas that should be reserved for Eli. But watching Daxton croon into that microphone during their final show in Houston made her knees quiver. The way his hand squeezed it, imagining the warmth of his breath against it, the close proximity to his lips…oh hell, was she really fantasizing about being a microphone to get closer to him? Her emotionally troubled *client*?

Yep. She was pretty much screwed. The guy had an excess of heart-melting layers. Seeing him with those kids, especially with Luke, God, it was almost impossible not to swoon, knowing he'd be the one to catch her. But the press only cared about the surface, nothing deeper. Superficial bullshit sold magazines and newspapers, and boosted television ratings. It was her job to remedy the public ills plaguing him and the rest of Jimmy Sixx, which meant keeping salacious thoughts to a minimum.

"You know, managers get their own private rooms. I've never been ridden on a tour bus before."

Sara let out a yelp as Eli's low voice vibrated against her ear. "Oh my gosh! You scared the hell out of me!"

"Why are you out here by yourself? We're not leaving for another half hour."

"I know. I was just trying to clear my head a little before the craziness starts." Yeah, that was it. Eradicate the carnal thoughts about a certain unattainable hot rocker before they compromised the ability to perform her job.

"So, what do you think? How about a quickie before we take off?" He wrapped his arms around her waist, the scent of his cologne swirling in the air around them. The spicy blend had never made her recoil before, but something about it now made her stomach roll.

"I don't think it's a good idea. Being here is such a big deal for a junior publicist. I have to make a good impression or word will get back to Jake and he'll pull me off the tour. I'm sure we'll have plenty of opportunities once things get rolling." She snickered. "No pun intended."

Eli let out a deep sigh and pulled away. "Fine, I get it."

"Don't be like that." Sara bit the inside of her mouth. Lusting after another guy and making guiltless, bullshit excuses to avoid the one she was supposed to be with was just wrong. But somehow, the security of being with Eli wasn't enough to sustain her emotional craving. She wanted what she couldn't have, what she shouldn't have, and it was dangerous with a capital D. "You know I can't just run off and—"

The back door of City Center Arena swung open. Hordes of people spilled out, flanked by mounds of luggage and equipment. Eli stepped back, immediately morphing from horn-dog-boy-toy to commandeering-badass. Oh well, better he channel the excess testosterone into his job instead of *her*.

"Techs, you have ten minutes to get everything loaded onto the bus. Head straight to the next venue and start on the setup. PAs, I need copies of all the rider checklists before you board the buses. There had better not be a single item missing from the green rooms in Dallas. If Laney's room smells of anything other than freesias, you're all fired." He turned toward Sara, his face now a mask of self-importance and control. "See you around." All business. No hug, no peck on the cheek. And dammit, if she wasn't a tiny bit relieved. As much as she hated to admit it, those weren't the lips she wanted brushing against her skin.

A cursory glance confirmed Eli had taken solace with his charges, one of whom was tall, tanned, and drop-dead gorgeous, with a half-hooded gaze that held enough heat to melt glaciers. Laney Taylor, the lead singer of Smeared Lipstick. An unfamiliar pang jolted Sara. Strange. It wasn't because of the way Eli was following her like a lovesick puppy with its tongue dragging on the concrete at her heels. Instead, flashbacks of the images plastered all over cyberspace flooded her mind. Laney and Daxton. Daxton and Laney. Laney, Daxton, and an unknown third party. Blech! Damned man-whore tendencies trumped everything else.

It wasn't her job to care about who or what he did, only to keep it out of the public eye. He could keep a freaking harem in his palatial suite on wheels for all she cared. Her stomach clenched. Nope, still not convincing enough.

Sara watched Laney's long, toned legs strut past and step onto the first bus in the line, a clingy black leather skirt barely covering her ass cheeks. No cellulite to be seen. Bitch. Eli almost tripped over himself trying to keep up. Sara stifled a snicker. Looked like he'd have his hands too full to worry about cornering her for hot tour bus sex.

"Sara."

She twisted in the direction of the voice, already

familiar with the condescending prick tone. "Hi, Merrick."

"Why are you out here? There are about fifty things that need to be done *inside* before we leave."

"What are you talking about? I'm a publicist, not your assistant. I've already taken care of everything that needs to be handled on my end. Aren't there PAs to handle *your* fifty things?"

The corners of Merrick's lips curled into a grimace. "If you're here, you'll do whatever the band requires. Right now, that includes getting their personal effects packed up and loaded onto the bus. If I were you, I'd get moving. And if you miss the bus, rest assured, you won't have to worry about catching another one."

What a freaking douchebag. She was there to make sure the guys kept their noses squeaky clean for the press. Period. Surely, he had plenty of other lackeys falling over themselves to tend to their every wish. "Listen, Merrick. I think there must be some misunderstanding. Jake made it clear that my responsibilities on this tour are limited to—"

He stepped closer, his dark eyes almost black. Unsettling. *Evil.* A chill snaked its way down her spine under his lewd stare. "That's what you still don't seem to understand. There *are* no limits, Sara."

Determined fingers gripped Daxton's backside, nails digging into the wet skin. She could lance the shit out of him for all he cared. His fingers tangled in her hair, his body thrusting deeper. Christ, her mouth was so hot and eager, so tight around him. She slurped like a champ, sucking his rock hard cock dry.

Fuck this.

He twisted the brass knob, letting out a groan as ice-cold water assaulted his back. Why should his balls be the only part of his anatomy that were blue? These sick and twisted fantasies about Sara were screwing with his head. Not being able to get off was becoming a major problem. Even imagining her on her knees, feasting on his dick, couldn't do the job anymore.

Knowing she was so close, imagining what lay beneath those sexy clothes after her body had been pressed against him, fantasizing about fucking her senseless on the back of the tour bus… it was a wonder he'd been able to perform a single song that night. Something about her had him turned inside out. She permeated every waking thought; merely picturing her tight little ass could have him hard in seconds.

He covered his face and let out a loud groan. Why couldn't he just rub one out like a normal fucking guy, for Christ's sake? Or at least slam some backup singer looking to get ahead in her career? What was it about Sara that had his head in a million different places? Or rather, *both* his heads…

That smart mouth of hers should have been screaming his name right about then, but besides her tool of a boyfriend, and the conflict of interest bullshit surrounding her job, he knew he'd ruin her. She was a good girl, not someone he needed to pull into his own downward spiral. All the slutty clothes in the world couldn't fool him. And he was bad, cold, empty, and void of everything she needed to find happiness. She knew it, too. That's why she'd left him the other night.

He turned off the shower and headed into the main area of his green room to air dry. His iPhone pinged, most likely with a text from Merrick telling him to get his ass moving. He was one of the privileged few who were allowed to deliver an order. Not that the orders were ever executed upon request.

A rustling sound made Daxton's brow furrow. His eyes adjusted to the dim glow of the wall sconces as he entered the room, now focused on the shapely ass bent over his duffel bag. Jean-clad, tight, begging to be grasped. *Hmm... familiar.*

"Looking for something?"

A high-pitched shriek pierced the air and the intruder spun around, long blonde hair fanning her face. His cock twitched. Of course, since it obviously only worked when Sara was around.

Her green eyes widened and she backed toward the door, her skinny boot heel catching in the shoulder strap of his bag. She gasped, grabbing onto the couch for leverage before planting face-first onto the plush carpet. "Jesus! Do you always sneak up on people when you're naked? Or am I the only privileged recipient of your sick and twisted peep show?"

He snickered and pulled on a pair of basketball shorts that were lying on a table. "I'm not used to finding unannounced visitors rummaging through my things. People usually knock before entering."

She folded her arms, nostrils flaring, fiery gaze darting in every direction. "Your head of security let me in."

"I'll fire Sean later."

"Don't do that! It wasn't his fault! I begged him because Merrick said I—"

"Relax, I was only kidding." He flopped onto the sofa, his body molding to the soft buttery leather. God, would he love to pull her on top of him and watch her ride his aching cock until he was finally sated. "Why are you so edgy?"

"You're supposed to be on the bus, and Merrick ordered me to come in here and pack your things to save time." She bent over the bag, stuffing it with clothes. That tasty ass beckoned again. Basketball shorts probably weren't the best choice to cover a half-hard on.

"Shouldn't one of the PAs be packing up?"

"Yes! There are only about ten of them strutting around here like they own the damned arena, acting like entitled little bitches. But yet, here I am, bent over your sweaty pile of clothes."

"I work hard on stage. Imagine what I can do when I'm only performing for one."

She jumped up. "I'm your freaking publicist, for chrissakes! Comments like that are what got you into trouble in the first place!"

He pushed back his still-damp hair, a teasing smirk lifting his lips. "Actually, I think it was the sex videos, but sure, we'll say it was the comments."

She narrowed her eyes. "I can't believe you're mocking me right now, when it's *your* career hanging by a string.

What the heck?"

"Stop packing the bag."

"I can't," she grumbled. "Merrick made it very clear that—"

"I'll take care of Merrick. Really. Just stop. It's not your job."

Sara held a black t-shirt between two fingers, scrunched her nose, and dropped it onto the pile. "Thank you. But you seriously need to get your life in order."

"I haven't done another sex video since the last one got leaked."

"You've missed multiple concert dates, been arrested for public intoxication and disorderly conduct three times in the past six months, and paraded more girls on and off your tour bus than there are days in a year."

"Wow. And I managed to write and record some songs in there, too. Go me."

Sara rolled her eyes. "This is serious."

"Agreed."

"Your reputation is in jeopardy."

"That's a little dramatic, don't you think?"

"Are you or are you not in danger of having your recording contract pulled?"

"I'm not exactly a menace to society. Even bad press is still good press."

"And based on events from the past few months, I can see why your former PR team has been fired. Maybe you should rethink that mantra."

He stretched his arms overhead, not bothering to mask the self-satisfied smile lifting his lips as her eyes raked over him. "I'll do whatever you want."

Stunned into silence. That was a first. Seemed like she never had a shortage of things to say. "Um…yeah, well, we uh…still need to review the rest of my plan."

"We could have done it the other night, but you chose to leave."

She ran a hand through her shiny blonde locks, dragging her eyes away. "We both know that's not why you asked me to stay."

Damned moonlight. It had messed with his head, made him say stupid things. But it wasn't just the moonlight. He'd opened up to her at a time when he was riddled with sadness. Her presence comforted him, filled the void, and he'd just wanted to hold on to those feelings for a bit longer; his reputation, however, always preceded him. No wonder she flew out of there so fast. "Maybe I just needed a friend."

"Maybe I was afraid you needed more than I could give." Her hand clenched the shoulder strap of his bag. "I'll just take this up to the bus."

He crossed the room in no more than three steps, covering her hand with his. Fuck, she smelled good, like the beach…sunshine, suntan lotion…her in a skimpy bikini or better yet, topless….

Her body stiffened against him. The duffel bag crashed to the floor.

"What if there were breakables in there? Are you going to be as careless with my tarnished reputation?" he breathed, her hair tickling the stubble lining his chin.

She twisted to face him, their lips only inches apart, fingers still entwined. A deep flush stained her cheeks. "I can't possibly do any more damage to it."

"You deserve more credit than that. Don't sell yourself short."

"Just so we're clear on roles, Daxton. I'm not the instigator here." She yanked her hand away and brushed past him, grasping the doorknob. "I'm the *fixer.*"

"...SHE JUST TOOK OFF...SOMETHING ABOUT A ghost...trying to hide...crazy shit."

"...never arrested...just disappeared...no trace?"

Merrick's voice floated into the hallway, but the other one was unfamiliar. He definitely wasn't shooting the breeze with one of the guys. Daxton inched closer to the door. It was cracked open, but he could only grab snippets of the conversation.

"She doesn't talk about it at all. Just wants to forget, I guess."

Who was the *she* they were talking about? Daxton's spine stiffened. What the hell about a ghost? Rage bubbled beneath the surface when Merrick's gruff voice grew louder. Just the sound made him want to pound the guy into next year.

"Take care, man. Let me know if you have any questions. I'm always around." Merrick appeared in the doorway, his eyes widening when they landed on Daxton. "Why the hell aren't you on the bus, man? We're about to take off."

Eli followed Merrick out the door. "Hey, Dax! Thanks again, Merrick. See you tomorrow."

Daxton nodded at Eli. If you can't say anything nice… just think it. *Fucking tool and his stupid hoodies. Converse. What a dick.* He glared at Merrick, waiting for Eli to be out of earshot. "Since when do you order my publicist to pack bags?"

Merrick pushed past him. "Come on, she was just wandering around looking useless and clueless. Isn't she here to learn the ropes? I was just trying to help."

"Really. And your brand of grunt work is teaching her how to be a more effective publicist?"

"Let's face it, she's not going to be much use to you with the press. May as well have her fill in the gaps."

"What the hell does that mean?"

"The girl comes from some Podunk town in the middle of nowhere. What the hell does she know about damage control and negotiating with the tabloids?"

"We both agreed she'd be an asset on the tour. Remember? Or has your brain half-melted away from all the shit you've been snorting?" Daxton's blood simmered as it coursed through his veins. "What the hell is your problem with her? You have a list of PAs that'll fuck you six ways to Sunday if you so much as blink in their direction. Why don't you leave Sara alone to do her job?"

Merrick's eyes glazed over. They were guarded and

unreadable, almost menacing. "Since when are you her protector? Shouldn't it be the other way around?"

"Leave her alone."

"What makes her so special, Dax? Huh? The fact that you haven't banged her yet?"

Daxton gritted his teeth. The blood rushing to his extremities was near boiling and ready to explode out of his ears like he was Old goddamned Faithful. "Stay the fuck away from her."

"You worry about your job, *rock star*, and let me do mine."

Approaching footsteps served as a warning to stand down. *Keep your fists locked before your ass gets thrown in jail for pummeling your best friend.*

"Something going on here?" Finn looked at Dax, then at Merrick.

"Nothing worth any more of my time." Jaw set, Daxton raked a hand through his hair. "I'll see you on the bus," he grunted before stalking down the hallway.

This girl. Dammit, she wrecked him, to the point where he was ready to flatten Merrick over a sweaty t-shirt. Defending her integrity seemed to be his new cause. How ironic he didn't give a crap about his own.

Talk about being blinded by lust. The sole image swimming in front of Sara's eyes was the one she'd just barely escaped... tanned, muscular chest, dark, penetrating gaze, and a rod that could act as a third leg. Beads of perspiration popped up along the back of her neck, her body temperature climbing with each passing second. Arousal pooled between her legs from the fantasy alone. Jesus, what else could he do with that mouth besides croon into a microphone?

Her calves burned with each step, but nothing could extinguish the tingling sensations swirling deep within her core, not even the agony of her toes being pinched together. She and Daxton had been only inches apart, and he smelled *so*…mmm. Heady, musky, and delicious. Alluring. Dangerous. Wrong! This whole thing was wrong on so many levels. Forget that the guy was like a Ferris wheel operator loading new passengers, one after another after yet *another*, never stopping, only slowing down to switch out patrons.

Click, click, click. Her stiletto heels clicked along the concrete in the direction of the buses. It was a feeble attempt to put as much distance between them as possible, when all she really wanted to do was rush back to the green room, fling herself into his damp embrace, and yank off those flimsy basketball shorts.

Get away as fast as you can! She grabbed the itinerary, squinting at it in the darkness. Where the hell was her bus waiting? The one where she'd be surrounded by a bunch of noisy roadies and PAs, far away from Daxton and all the crazy erotic thoughts polluting her mind, like the one where she was on her back, writhing beneath him in a king-sized bed so fluffy and plush it felt like they were literally screwing on cloud nine? Yeah. All of those images needed to be eradicated, and a new memory chip was needed desperately; either that, or a lobotomy before breakfast.

Her buzzing iPhone was the only discernable sound in the now vacant arena corridor. Her fingers closed around it, squeezing, praying...

You can't hide because I'll always find you. I will make you pay for what you did.

Tears pooled in her eyes, and the urge to flee grabbed hold, choking her until she was barely able to draw in a single breath. Somehow, he'd found her. But how? Only Eli knew she'd fled Grand Falls, and she never told him the reason for her rapid departure. Running was always the preferred option, although it had proven to be pretty ineffective to date. How foolish of her to think a clear escape would solve her problems and give her what she so craved: a new beginning, safe from harm, away from the demons on a perpetual hunt to track her every movement? And what was she searching for? Freedom? Redemption? A chill zipped through her when she emerged from the tunnel, the cool, crisp air a harsh reminder of that fateful night. How she'd shivered in the moonlight, alone, afraid, and *guilty*.

So much for protection. Nobody could help her, not Eli, not her parents. Her fate was in the hands of another, yet again. Except this time, she had no idea who she was running from. And when she was caught, would anyone be there to save her?

ELEVEN

"OKAY GUYS, LET'S GET STARTED." Daxton's pick flew over the guitar strings to start the intro, the others joining in. An early sound check, after a fitful night on the bus, was not an ideal way to start the day. He was grouchy, hung over, and anchored with a massive case of blue balls.

After the first bar, a loud screech reverberated between his ears, making him yank out the earpiece. "Ahh! What the fuck?"

"Uh, Dax, sorry about that." Jim, the head technician, fiddled with the amplifiers set up on stage. "These cables are all messed up. We're gonna have to rework the system before the show tonight."

Daxton let out a deep sigh, bleary-eyed from a lack of sleep and excess of Jack. Too much time fantasizing with not nearly enough action. Christ, he needed to get off. His eyes darted around the darkened arena, searching, hoping…to no avail. Sara was nowhere to be found. His cock twitched, making him stifle a groan. He was a goddamn rock star and could have as much pussy as he wanted at any given time. Yet, here he was, pining for his junior publicist, who'd made it pretty damned clear that she was off limits.

Game fucking *on*.

If only that toolbox of a boyfriend didn't keep skulking around like she was a raw steak and he was a ravenous lion. What a dickhead.

His head still throbbed from the shriek of the speakers. Or maybe it was from all of the booze. "Finn, where the hell are the PAs? I need Advil. And some fries with mustard."

Finn pointed to the exit sign with his drumstick. "Probably getting coffee or some shit. Maybe Merrick has them setting up the green rooms." He tapped his cymbal. "Too much fun last night with your hand?"

"Screw you." Dax collapsed onto a stool. "The only thing clutched in my hand was a shot glass."

"So that's why you're in such a sparkly mood." Finn tossed him a bottle of water. "Drink this. Let it flush out the booze."

The cool water drenched his bone-dry throat. At least he wouldn't be croaking like a damn frog when the sound system was finally up and running. Running. Maybe that's what he needed. Endorphins. Another gulp of water landed in his empty stomach. Fuck that. He needed food.

Jim emerged from backstage holding a bunch of wires. "Guys, I need to test all these. The connections are down.

Let's regroup in thirty, okay? I'll send the crew for you."

"Yeah, that's fine, Jim." Daxton clapped him on the back. "We have faith in you." He pulled out his phone to text Merrick and shuffled past Cooper, not bothering to lift his head. If he made eye contact, there was a pretty big chance he'd end up pounding the shit out of the guy right there on stage.

"Dax."

He shrugged off Cooper's hand, not slowing his gait. "Busy."

"Come on, man. We need to talk."

"We definitely *should* have talked." He turned, eyes narrowed. "Before you acted. It's too late now. Too fucking late."

"It doesn't have to be." Cooper inched closer, a pained expression on his face. He looked like shit. Dark circles hung below his eyes, stubble lined his pale face, and his hair was mussed. If he hadn't known better, he'd have thought Cooper had been screwing some groupie all night.

"Dax!" Merrick called from backstage. "I gotta talk to you."

"Leave it alone, Coop. Just…fucking leave it alone." Daxton ran a hand through his thick hair as he walked off stage toward Merrick.

"What's up, Q?"

"You look like crap, man. Did you sleep at all?"

"I've got a lot of shit on my mind these days."

"I know you're worried about Luke. Have you heard anything?"

"Nothing new." He'd called every day since that last

visit, and although Luke's spirits were up, it was only a matter of time before the tides changed. They always did.

"Let me know if you need me to do anything." Merrick cleared his throat. "Listen Dax, about last night—"

"Forget it. I said what I had to say. Just don't let it happen again."

"Okay. It's done." Merrick waved a pink Post-It at him. "I hate to pile on, but Gracie called."

Daxton let out a groan. Gracie, as in his father's PA. Great, because this day just couldn't get any better. "Call your father asap." Short, most definitely not sweet. He crumpled the paper into a tight ball and flung it into a nearby trash can.

"So you're not calling."

"Nope."

"It's probably about the wedding."

"Then let me change my answer. Hell fucking no."

"Want me to take care of it?"

"Nothing to take care of." Dax guzzled the remaining water. "Except my breakfast, which I hope is waiting in my green room."

"Yes, Your Majesty. I'll get right on it."

The message had pissed him off, but seeing Merrick bow with a flourish cracked his asshole veneer. He smirked. "Since you offered, make the bacon well-done this time, or I'm finding a new lackey."

"Too bad your personality chases them away within the first hour of meeting you." Merrick grinned.

"I'm going to crash. Let me know when we're a go for the sound check." Daxton grabbed his vibrating phone.

Unknown number. After all this time, hope never completely deserted him. Only a handful of people had this number, one of which had pulled a disappearing act almost a year ago. And every day since then, he'd held on to the possibility that she might resurface. His fingers couldn't click Accept fast enough. "Yeah?"

"Daxton, I have your father for you." Fuck. Gracie. Of course Tyler would resort to the blocked number bullshit.

"Think you can keep your dick in your pants until after the wedding? I don't want anything overshadowing this for Layla, especially your extracurricular activities." Tyler's voice dripped with disdain.

"Hey, Dad. Great to hear from you. Yeah, I'm doing okay, thanks for asking. Just got over a cold, but hey, life goes on, right?"

Greeted with silence. Guess there was a first time for everything.

"Cut the sarcasm. It's a big day for her."

"Oh, is it her first wedding? And her parents are okay with it? They signed the marriage certificate for her and everything?"

"I don't appreciate your attitude. And I'm expecting you at the ceremony. Gracie faxed the details."

"Yeah, you know, I think I'm busy that day. Besides, aren't you still weirded out that the tabloids claimed that I fucked your future wife before you did? Those rumors still keeping you up at night?" He drained the last of the water and slammed the bottle on a nearby table.

"Daxton, I want you there. You should be there. Much as you hate it, I'm still your father."

"Oh, I don't hate *it*, Dad."

"Don't disrespect me."

"You don't give a shit about getting respect from me. Every move you make is a ploy to hold onto that spotlight. And let's face it, you don't take kindly to anyone who steals it away." He clicked off the phone and shoved it into his back pocket. The heaviness in his heart weighed on him like a cement brick. His father was the only real family he had left, and he couldn't have felt more alone. Abandoned by his mother, rejected by his father, and survived longer than his only brother, the best friend he could ever hope to have.

"Hey, Dax."

He raised his eyes to meet bright blue ones staring back. Gia Lourdes, drummer for Smeared Lipstick. Gorgeous, tall, and curves for years.

A long, purple lacquered nail trailed his bicep. "Heard you guys had a few technical issues. Wanna kill some time?"

He scoured the hallway. Still no sign of Sara. His eyes flicked back toward Gia. Long, blonde hair streamed down her scantily clad back. *Yeah, why the hell not? Just bang her from behind. She could be anyone.*

As long as he could fool his dick into believing that.

TWELVE

"Jake, I didn't agree to come on this tour so I could be a lackey. I really want to establish myself, and I—"

"Listen, Sara. You wanted a chance to grow your career? This is it. When they say jump, your only response should be how high. Period. If you want out, say the word, and we'll send someone in your place. But if you bail, just know there won't be another opportunity waiting in the wings for a junior PR rep with a diva complex."

Argh! She clenched her fists, nails practically drawing blood. "How am I supposed to get experience if I'm packing up their dirty laundry when I should be interacting with the press?"

"It's all about making the band happy. If they're happy, I'm happy. If I'm happy, you get more big name clients. See how that works?"

"Fine, but I really don't see how that's helping—"

"My next appointment is here. Just focus on making sure they like you and that they're flying under the radar, especially Daxton Cole. Guy is a loose cannon and any more bad press will bury him, and the rest of Jimmy Sixx will come crumbling down around his corpse."

She let out a deep sigh. *Great, sweaty underwear, here I come.*

"Okay, I'll be—"

Click.

"In touch."

Jake may have owned one of the biggest PR firms in the country, but what a freaking douchebag.

"Hey, gorgeous." Strong arms wound around her waist, and for a split second, she let the belief it was Daxton take hold. The wet, soaped up, naked version that had commanded her thoughts for the better part of the last hour. "Let's get dinner. Better yet, let's skip dinner and go straight to dessert." Eli backed her against the wall of the arena, burying his head in her neck. It was probably supposed to be sexy, seductive, alluring, and something remotely resembling hot, at the very least. But while his hungry tongue lapped incessantly at her ear, all she could think of was Daxton's full, kissable lips and how they'd feel pressed against her skin.

"Eli." She twisted away, cringing at the moisture gathered on her earlobe and neck. *Gross.*

"What's the matter?" His blue eyes narrowed. "We finally get the chance to be alone in my hotel on wheels and you're not in the mood?"

"I'm sorry. Today has been really frustrating. Jake is pissing me off, Merrick is acting like a tool and..." *And Gia is probably screwing Daxton Cole senseless right about now and dammit, I wish it was me!* An icy sensation snaked around her heart and squeezed. What the heck was her problem? Eli was a good guy – attentive, affectionate, handsome – and any girl would be excited to be with him. Any girl, it seemed, but her, because her sights were set on the guy who couldn't manage to keep his pants zipped. The same guy who didn't give a damn about his own livelihood, or anything more permanent than a few salacious hours.

Was it really that hard of a choice? Or was it a choice at all?

G IA LOURDES. OF COURSE, DAXTON
would pick her for a quick lay. She was exactly his
type—huge tits, great ass, one-syllable vocabulary.
Fucking skank.

Meandering the dimmed corridors, skulking around columns, trying to catch even a glimpse of how this tortured rock god operated when he thought nobody else was watching, obsessing about every inch of his hard, sculpted body, and how it would feel plastered against—

Fuck! What kind of sick, crazed person did that shit?

A lump the size of a golf ball took up residence, shallow breaths barely able to squeeze through as muffled sounds of Gia's wailing carried into the desolate hallway. Even with eyes squeezed shut, the images kept looping, over and over, in excruciatingly lewd detail.

Shocking realization had long since turned into full-on obsession.

Unrequited love was a real bitch, accidental though it was.

Speaking of which, it looked like Gia might be due for an accident herself...

EAT EMITTED BY THE FLASHING strobe lights was always unbearable, but tonight, it was suffocating. Sweat dripped down Daxton's back, drenching through the black t-shirt as his hands raced over the guitar strings. He squinted through the drops of perspiration burning his eyes. After a few more breathless notes, the final bridge was in sight. Almost time to put this day far behind him, burying it for good. Christ, how jaded had he become that the one thing he loved more than anything had become so stifling?

Once the curtain fell, he expelled a deep sigh, which released exactly none of the angst gripping him. Even an hour with Gia writhing against him, naked, wet, and ready, couldn't get him hard. She sucked, rubbed, and tugged to no avail. Every attempt to put Sara out of his mind was futile, and now, with all the media hype surrounding his father's upcoming nuptials to that mindless bimbo, Layla, there wasn't a hope or prayer for reconstruction of his emotional state. The press just loved any excuse to tear open all of his old wounds - Jase, Cooper, his mother. His mind knew he needed to move on, but dammit, his heart ignored every plea. How much longer could he just stand still?

"Dax, Kayla and Gia were talking about staying on the bus tonight. You want me to take care of that? Or do you have someone else in mind for your post-show entertainment? I figured it would be good to mingle with our openers, yeah?" Finn slung an arm around his shoulders then recoiled. "Fuck, man, you're disgusting!"

"Nobody told you to start pawing at me, dude." Daxton ran a hand through his sweat-soaked hair. "And not tonight. I'm hitting it hard and *alone*."

"Porn? Seriously?" Finn nodded toward the crowd of women waving various articles of lingerie in the air. "Take your pick. I can have any of those freaky chicks spread eagle on your bed in five minutes."

"No, I'm hitting the *pillow*, Finn. I'm exhausted. But feel free to enjoy your threesome."

"I may need to take them to my green room before we ship out. Two chicks in my bunk on the bus isn't going to work. At least, not for the other guys. I needed your sweet suite." Finn flashed a wicked grin at Daxton before giving his arm a hard punch. "Have fun *sleeping*."

Daxton grabbed a bottle of water from a table backstage. Finn joined Cooper and Liam, who were surrounded by paparazzi. Incessant camera flashes antagonized the stress knot sitting at the base of his skull. Scantily clad girls - not women, *girls*; most not more than twenty - waited eagerly in a roped off area, hoping to be fingered by one of the band members, and invited to a raucous after party.

He wasn't in the mood. Seemed like he'd been saying that way too much lately. What the hell kind of rock star was he anyway? Mooning after one girl when there were thousands of others who'd give a limb to share his bed?

Merrick emerged from the throng of spectators, a look of concern on his face. "You okay?"

"As good as can be expected."

"Finn said you don't want to get laid tonight. Do you feel sick or something? Want me to call a doctor?"

Daxton barked out a laugh. "I'm *fine*. Just tired, though I appreciate the concern about my alleged diminished sex drive."

"You're sure you don't want me to pick anyone out?"

"One hundred and fifty percent sure. I need sleep." With any luck, he'd escape the nightmares. Booze always helped numb his mind enough to settle. Without it, who knew what demons would be chasing him? Fuck it, he'd take the risk. The ills ailing him couldn't be remedied with alcohol *or* sex, and it was about time he'd accepted that and figured out how to come to terms with everything clouding his life.

"*After* you shower."

"After I shower." Dax rolled his eyes. "Now, get me out of here."

Merrick waved over a couple of the bodyguards. "Guys, can you clear a path?"

"Back to the bus, Dax?" Sean, the larger of the two, and the band's head of security, asked. Yes, he was actually bigger, if that was even believable, considering both were built like brick shithouses on stilts.

"Yeah." He gulped the last remaining droplets of water, draining the bottle. The bulky guys huddled around him, making sure none of the rowdy and grabby females sunk their claws into him. It was like a gauntlet, except instead of knives being flung at him, it was fake tits. And if you've felt one, well, everyone knows the rest of that line. Now, Sara's rack was one he'd wished was being offered. Lush, perky, sans silicone. Those babies pressed against him... fuck yeah, sleep would lose in that competition.

Where was she, anyway? Daxton's neck craned back toward the crowd still hovering around the rest of the band. Sara's blonde hair fanned out behind her as she twisted in the direction of a reporter, no doubt trying to salvage Daxton's reputation. It was a tough job, though he'd like to personally make sure it wasn't a thankless one. Except she was a good girl, with a boyfriend, and she was well aware of how much of a disaster he was. Just a few tiny obstacles cock blocking him.

Sean led the way down the corridor, away from the roadies breaking down sets, away from the shrieking fans and flying bras and panties...and Sara. No party for him. Maybe he really did need some therapy.

"Excuse me, Daxton Cole?"

Jolted from his reverie, Daxton turned slightly in the direction of the voice. It was a man, about forty, with dark hair and dark eyes, and a little shorter than he.

Sean turned around, lowering his voice. "You know this guy, Dax?"

"No, keep moving."

As requested, they directed him toward the buses, faster now that they had a new and unwelcome audience.

"Please wait. I just want to talk to you for a minute."

"You heard him. He doesn't know you. Leave now." Alex, the other guard, palmed his gun. "Trust me, this isn't a toy."

"I don't want any trouble. I just…if I could just get a *second…*"

The hairs on the back of Daxton's neck stood at attention. He paused to look back at the man wringing his hands. What kind of sick fuck was tailing him now? Of course, there had been others. There always were. But somehow this one had gotten in close.

Sean positioned himself behind Dax, his size enough to block anyone from breaching the perimeter. "Don't worry, we'll take care of him. You need anything else, Dax?"

Daxton's eyes flickered back toward Alex and where he'd backed the guy against the side of the arena, using his massive weight to muscle him. There was something so familiar about the guy, creepy as he was.

He started up the steps, but the man's next words uttered in what sounded like pure desperation, paralyzed any future movement.

"I knew your mother."

N O ANSWER. OF COURSE NOT, IT WAS
Saturday night. Sara let out a deep sigh.
What was she thinking? The mayor of Grand
Falls and his socialite wife would no doubt be pouring
themselves into bed around dawn after schmoozing at
some fundraising event. Why should they be bothered with
their only daughter, the one they'd exiled?

It wasn't like they could really do anything to help her,
beyond pulling strings to get her into this PR firm. She was
on her own now, and yeah, it still scared the crap out of
her, especially since receiving those texts. Someone knew.
Someone was angry. And someone was freaking her the
heck out.

The crowds surrounding Finn, Cooper, and Liam
eventually dispersed, and the guys made their way back to

the tour bus with some parting gifts and their respective owners. Jeez, it was like a big orgy.

She swallowed a gasp. *Holy cow.*

One glaring fact was that Daxton was nowhere in sight. After the show ended, he'd bee lined for the exit – no hassles, no groupies, no time wasted. Was he waiting on the bus already? Was he the orchestrator of this whole sex fest? It would be really helpful to know what tabloid headlines she might wake up to in the morning, and what kind of damage control would be required to hang on to her job. Freaking horny rock stars and their obscene lifestyles. Freaking Daxton Cole and his ability to turn her inside out with the flash of those delicious brown eyes.

A chill zipped through her. Stupid denim jacket had more strategically placed holes than a slice of Swiss cheese. Stylish and trendy? Yes. Practical? Heck, no. She gripped it tightly around her, teeth chattering. Except it wasn't the temperature that had her stomach in knots and her mind projecting very X-rated films starring her and Daxton.

This obsession, inane as it was, had to end. But that wasn't the only thing.

A quick text to Eli yielded no response after a few minutes. Everyone should be accounted for by now. The itinerary said they'd soon be heading to the next venue. And this couldn't wait a second longer. Chest tight, she found herself standing at the entrance of the bus carrying the Smeared Lipstick crew members. Darn it, she'd always hated this part.

She stepped on board, scanning the interior. Lots of faces, none were Eli's. *Where the heck could he be?*

"Need something, sweetheart?" A tall, lanky guy with glasses leered at her.

"Um, yes. I'm looking for Eli Maclane."

The guy nodded past her. "Room's at the back of the bus."

"Thanks." She took a deep breath. Nobody paid attention as she squeezed past. Loud music blared from the speakers, while multiple plasma screens were displaying some kind of video game. Violent ones, from the looks of them. Lots of guns and blood. Bullets popped and grenades exploded. It was hard to think amidst the noise. Maybe that was a good thing, considering she was about to pull the rug out from under the poor guy. But it wasn't fair to lead him on anymore. Not when she couldn't stop thinking about another. She wasn't in it, and he needed to know.

After a few knocks with no response, most likely due to an inability to hear, she grasped the door handle and pushed it open.

And God, did she ever wish she could unsee what was in her direct line of sight.

She'd recognize that hair anywhere. Full, blonde curls bounced over the shoulders of one Laney Taylor, as her tanned, naked body rode Eli like a paperboy on a bike trying to escape a vicious dog attack.

A sharp intake of breath sliced into Sara's lungs. Her limbs were frozen, immobile. The sight was like a runaway train heading toward a tree at two hundred miles per hour. Her eyes refused to move, and her mouth was temporarily on strike. Not the best time to be rendered mute. *Argh! Say something, damnit!*

All at once, she'd regained the ability to speak. Well, yell, actually.

"You scumbag!"

Eli's eyes popped open wide. "Sara!"

Laney shrieked, jumping off Eli and wrapping herself in a sheet. "What the hell is wrong with you? Don't you knock?"

"Don't you make sure the guys you're going to screw don't already have girlfriends? Or is this supposed to be a case of 'well, sweetie, she was on my list, so it really doesn't count'?" Sara glared at Eli. "Because it does, you asshole!"

"You have a girlfriend?" Laney grabbed her sweatshirt and pulled it over her now-mussed hair. "And she's part of the tour?"

"Yes, but I—I—"

"You what, Eli? You are just a total waste of space!" Sara glanced at Laney, who was hopping on one foot to pull on her leggings. "Keep him. I'm done."

Laney's high-pitched voice, endlessly spewing expletives, pierced her brain as she pushed past the open-mouthed spectators gathered outside of Eli's door. What a lying, cheating bastard! That was an unanticipated twist, albeit a welcome one. Good riddance. She wasn't some shrinking violet, ready to bend over at a moment's notice to satisfy anyone. This was the beginning of a new chapter; the one where she called the shots and was ready to kick ass... if there were asses needing to be kicked.

SIXTEEN

"DAX, WHERE THE HELL ARE YOU going?" Finn's question was followed by a yawn so loud, it could have woken the inhabitants of the neighboring buses. "We have sound check in an hour."

Daxton ran a hand through his tousled, gel-crunched hair and pulled on a Houston Astros baseball cap. "I'm going for a run."

"Sorry, I don't speak that language. Come again?"

"I need to clear my head, okay? Buy me some time. I'll be back."

"Since when do you run? Don't you want to get breakfast instead? Bacon, egg, and cheese sandwich, home fries, *coffee*?"

"Look, it was a shitty night. I need to get out for a while.

Alone."

"Dude, Merrick is gonna—"

"He'll deal. I'll see you later."

Daxton slid open the tour bus door, breathing in the crisp, fresh air. Nobody in sight. Great, he finally had a chance to escape the questions he couldn't answer, questions he didn't even want to acknowledge.

The sun peeked over the clouds as he sank into a hamstring stretch. His muscles were so tight, just like the knot that had taken up residence at the base of his skull. Ironic. Excessive booze normally had the opposite effect. And he'd pretty much drank himself sober after last night's debacle. How the hell had that guy gotten so close?

He rubbed the back of his neck, desperate to relieve the knot. "Dammit!"

"Rough night?"

That raspy voice made him jump about twenty feet into the air. Christ, did she know how sexy her voice sounded in the morning? He'd love to hear it waking him up after a very sleepless night infused with lots of carnal pleasures. *Oh, fuck yeah.*

"I didn't mean to startle you." Sara twirled her ponytail around her index finger, a sleepy smile on her face. The soft morning light danced atop her head, half-hooded green eyes making his cock twitch. Shit, even at this ungodly hour of the morning?

"I didn't expect anyone else to be awake."

"Thought you'd escape unnoticed, huh?" Sara smirked. "I'm going for a run. Figured it was my only chance for some peace and quiet before Merrick assigns me his list of errands for the day."

"Uh-huh." His eyes raked over the curves poured into hot pink spandex, mind unable to formulate a thought beyond peeling her out of those constricting clothes. Immediately, if not sooner.

"Okay, then."

"Okay, what?"

She grabbed her ankles one at a time, pulling each toward to her perfect ass, stretching her quads. "Let's go. You shouldn't be by yourself, anyway."

"So you're gonna protect me?"

Her pink lips curled into a sly smile. "It's my job. Now stop procrastinating and *move*."

"You're kind of pushy. Why can't we ease into it? Nice and slow to start?"

"Nice and slow, huh? Kind of shocking. You don't seem the type."

He stretched his arms over his head. "I don't know what you're implying. I was talking about *running*."

"Sure you were." She tightened her ponytail. "Trust me, you'll feel better once you sweat out all the alcohol."

A slow trot increased in intensity much too quickly, and soon, they were circling the arena parking lot at full speed. *Focus, focus, focus!* His primary objective was not to collapse. A sidelong glance confirmed Sara had barely broken a sweat since they'd started. No words were exchanged, which was a good thing, since he couldn't catch a single breath. A burning sensation erupted in the pit of his belly, spreading through his lungs, singeing his insides. His legs, now feeling more like Jell-O than actual limbs, were on the brink of revolution. Why didn't he grab a bottle of water? Panting only made his mouth drier, as if it wasn't already more arid than the Sahara at midday. Sweat drizzled into his eyes, blurring his vision. How many more times were they going to make this death loop?

Sara pivoted to face him, tiny beads of perspiration glistening along her hairline, the only sign she was exerting herself at all. Jogging backwards. Not even changing her gait. He was a step above pathetic – a very short step.

"How is it that you can't even make it a mile without looking like you're about to pass out?"

Great, he needed to speak now?

"It's not like…I'm…Britney Spears…shaking my ass… all over the stage." His calf muscles ached as his sneakers pounded the pavement. Bacon, egg, and cheese had been a very delicious alternative, and he opted out for this self-inflicted torture? "I play guitar…and sing…doesn't require… cardio." He mopped his face with the edge of the t-shirt. "How the hell…are you…able to do this? I don't think… your boy…friend is…keeping you…up late…enough."

Croaking out those last words nearly killed him, for multiple reasons.

"You should really consider traveling with an oxygen mask." She flipped around, giving him a glimpse of her shapely backside, just about the only thing keeping him going. "And, just so you know, he's not my boyfriend anymore."

"Not your…boy—" A sharp pain shot through his foot, stopping him mid-stride. "Ahh!" His body rocketed forward, arms flailing, sending him to the pebbly concrete lot with nothing to cushion the blow except his pride.

Thump!

"Holy crap, are you okay?" Sara fell to the ground where he was writhing in agony, bits of pebble mashed into his skin. "Where does it hurt?"

He let out a loud groan and fell backward. "Fuck. Everywhere!"

"Do you think anything's broken?" Her hand squeezed his and for the briefest of seconds, the presence of his very intense pain faded, replaced by Sara's compassion, worry, and genuine concern. Somebody actually cared. That hadn't happened in…shit, long enough that he couldn't pinpoint an amount of time. It felt nice. Until the agony crashed over him again like a tsunami.

Sitting up was a struggle, but dammit, he was already hovering on the brink of being a complete and total pansy ass. *Ignore the pain. Find out what happened with the boyfriend.* Even a fall like that couldn't quell his curiosity. He had to know, even if he was going to be in traction and unable to do anything about it for the foreseeable future.

"Am I allowed to ask what happened?"

A look of shock flitted across Sara's face, quickly followed by a snicker. "Wow. Your focus is impressive, even with four potentially broken limbs." Her playful tone couldn't mask her nerves, though. She toyed with her ponytail again, normally bright green eyes darkening. "I walked in to find Laney riding him like she was competing for the Triple Crown."

"Horse racing fan?"

"Yeah, we have a horse farm back home. Raised several

thoroughbreds. I always loved to ride." She averted her eyes, but not before he caught a glimpse of what she'd been trying to shield.

"Where's home?"

"Minnesota." She sat back on her heels, eyes still guarded. Conversation over. "So, what do you think? Are you able to hoof it back to the buses?"

"Eli is a fucking idiot."

A slow smile brightened her flushed face. "Agreed." She held out a hand. "Come on, let's see if those legs still work."

"Are you gonna carry me if they don't?"

"You don't pay me enough."

Gritting his teeth, he pulled himself to his feet. "Christ, I feel like I've been run over by a freight train."

Sara snaked an arm around his waist, hoisting him against her. "Take it slow, okay? You said you liked that."

The scent of citrus wafted into the air between them. So delicious, like a fruit salad. How could she still smell so good after that run? "Yeah…I figured you'd use that against me soon enough."

"Can I ask you something?"

"Looks like we have lots of time to kill before we make it back to camp. Shoot."

"What happened last night? Who was the guy?"

"I don't know what you're talking about." *How the hell did she even know?*

"I'm sure your little groupies love the coy act, but I'll pass." She cocked an eyebrow. "Daxton, I'm part of your PR team. It's my job to know everything that goes on during this tour. Sean from security told me someone approached you. I can't do damage control without all the facts. Who was he, and what did he want? Or, maybe a better question might be *what does he know*?"

His face twisted into a grimace with each step. The buses weren't even in sight. With any luck, they'd make it back by lunchtime. "You ever feel like you're suffocating? That there's air all around, but you just can't breathe it in? Like your body resists what it needs to survive, and you feel like you're constantly drowning? That's how I feel most of the time. The air, everything around me – what people see, what they want to believe, judgments they make based on half-truths – it's all toxic. Better not to inhale. The lesser of two evils, but either way, I'm fucked."

She nodded, her hair tickling his shoulder. "I do know what you mean." Her voice was soft, *sad*. There was something beneath that snarky exterior, something he was desperate to uncover, but her demeanor begged him not to press.

They walked for a few silent minutes that seemed to stretch into hours. He clenched and unclenched his fists as waves of pain assaulted his ankle. "Shit, that hurts."

"I don't think you should push it. Let me call Merrick."

"No." He stopped, teetering on one leg. "Please. Not yet. Can we just sit down for a minute?"

"Of course." She eased him to the ground and sank onto the pavement. "Is there anything I can—?"

"The guy from last night said he knew my mother." Daxton held his head, expelling a deep breath. "She disappeared after my brother died last year, without a trace. Without a warning. One day, she was there; the next, gone.

With her clothes, car, jewelry. Everything…gone. My dad made a half-hearted attempt to find her, but I was too angry to try. I'd just lost my best friend, and my mother picked that time to bail. We should have been there for each other, but she didn't care enough to even say goodbye."

"I'm so sorry." Sara grasped his hand. Her skin was so soft against his calloused fingers. It was an occupational hazard for a guitarist.

"I don't want to have anything to do with her. She abandoned her family. Things between her and my dad were never great, but what the hell did I ever do to her?"

"So you had security get rid of him."

"People always have an angle, Sara." He raised his eyes to see the empathy reflected in her gaze. "I can't trust anyone because everyone has an agenda. They want to know what I can do for them, how much I'll pay to keep something from happening, what they can hold over my head in exchange for things they want. Even if this guy is telling the truth, I'm not willing to listen because nothing comes without a high price tag. *Toxic*. But the problem is, even though my body tries to protect me by resisting the urge to inhale the poison around me, I want to live, to be whole again, free from all this useless anger and resentment. I need to breathe." He raked a hand through his hair. "I just can't remember how."

SEVENTEEN

CAMERA FLASHES WERE BLINDING AS shutters clicked and whirred, the medic wheeling a very bruised and bloodied Daxton into the back entrance of the arena. It was near impossible to stand down and watch Sara fawning over him when being wrapped in Daxton's muscular arms was the only place—

Goddammit! He'd chosen Sara. Again. What the hell did he see in her? Skin-tight spandex, slut-ass clothes, no ability to assert herself. She couldn't possibly satisfy him. She'd probably never even seen a dick before, much less sucked one. No, Daxton needed more. So much more...

The urge to yank Sara by the hair and claw out her stupid Bambi eyes was overpowering. But that would screw up the plan, tempting as it was. No, patience was a necessity. In the end, true love would always conquer all.

Daxton is mine. It's only a matter of time until he realizes it, too.

EIGHTEEN

SARA PACED THE MAIN AREA OF THE GREEN room, her stomach in knots. Scrapes and scratches were nothing compared to her own inner turmoil stewing below the surface. Hearing Daxton's words, laced with pain, seeing the dejection on his face…good God, it was heart wrenching and shocking to witness, considering how the world, including her, had judged so harshly without knowing him at all.

She drew in a deep breath, a futile attempt to calm her pulse. *Stop thinking about his naked, soaped up body, and find the first-aid kit!* A frantic tear through the room confirmed the only alcohol available was in glass bottles. And a few shots of whatever the heck it was might be necessary right then.

A loud ping sent her stumbling into the couch. Darn

it. It was Kat, the record label's social media director. Sara had barely exchanged two words with the woman since they started back up in Houston. Kat was a master at online damage control and spent most of her time on a mobile device of some sort. *What the hell happened to Dax? Do you have a press conference scheduled?*

Really? A flipping press conference? Jesus. The guy hadn't even finished showering. The press really was relentless. The world just could not get enough of Daxton Cole, and any story was newsworthy, including a fall in an arena parking lot.

The running water stopped. Her stomach clenched. He was naked, alone, and *wet*. Sweet Lord, she was going straight to hell with the X-rated thoughts wallpapering her mind.

A loud crash followed by a string of expletives made her jump, yanking her from the private porno on permanent loop. "Dax?" She crept toward the bathroom door, chewing her lower lip. "Are you okay?"

"The word okay is relative."

"Do you want me to get someone?"

He let out a deep sigh. "No, but can you help me? Don't worry, I'm decent."

Too bad. She rolled her eyes. What was wrong with her? The door creaked open. Daxton stood in front of the white pedestal sink, squeezing a deep red-stained towel around his left hand. Her eyes widened. "Oh my God! You're bleeding. What happened?"

"Damned shelf collapsed and the jar of cotton shattered. I sliced my finger when I was picking up the pieces."

She grabbed a box of Band-Aids from a nearby cabinet. The gash wasn't deep. A few Band-Aids and a little Neosporin, and his hand was good as new.

"Thanks."

"Maybe you need a new PA after all." Tiny shards of glass were scattered across the tile floor. "Come on, I'll help you get out of here. Let's at least try to keep your feet intact."

He let out a groan. "Can this day get any worse?"

"You're still alive, so you haven't exactly hit rock bottom yet. And I need to organize a press conference to announce your status to the world, according to Kat. Evidently, the Internet is already blowing up." She slid an arm around his waist. "Be careful. If you slip, you'll take us both down."

"Would that be a terrible thing?"

Warmth spread throughout her core. *Mmm, no. Not at all.* His arm tightened around her. She tensed, twisting toward him. God, he smelled so good, soapy clean and manly. Good enough to lick. Oh shoot, what was happening? He was sad, upset, and needy. She couldn't...*wouldn't* be that girl; the stupid one who thought this might actually mean anything to him. But his dark-eyed gaze held her captive, rooted to the spot, and made her tingle in all the wrong places. Running was simply not an option.

"Sara..." He pulled her close, his pepperminty-scented breath tickling her cheeks. It was impossible to think; the sound of her thundering heart drowned out all conscious thought. His lips crushed against hers - demanding, hungry, *desperate*. They were so soft, so perfect, and better than she'd imagined. A delicious ache between her legs grew more intense with each passing second.

115

The sensations coursing through her could make her swoon on the spot and he'd barely touched her. No, this was wrong. So wrong, on way too many levels. They had to stop. She raised her hands, knowing she needed to push him away, but her body wouldn't obey.

But, mmm, his devilish tongue had other ideas, more salacious ones that told a very carnal story in which she played a key role. It coiled around hers, devouring the fledgling doubts cropping up in her mind. Wrong, but so flipping *good*.

She ran her fingers through his damp hair, trailing them down his muscular arms, and over his perfectly chiseled torso - a god in every sense of the word.

"Dax! You in there?"

Sara swallowed a yelp, stumbling backward into a wall. Her breaths came in short gasps. "Shoot, what just…oh my God…I can't believe—"

He silenced her by laying a finger over her mouth. "Q, I'll be out in a minute."

Silence. Sara's heart almost stopped. If Merrick had come in and found her in here, her big shot would come to a screeching halt. He'd send her packing before lunch. A reluctant response followed. "Okay. See you in a few."

Daxton tucked a loose strand of hair behind her ear. "What's wrong?"

Her eyes popped open wide. "Are you seriously asking me that? We just kissed, and you—"

"Really enjoyed it." A smirk lifted the corners of those scrumptious lips. He leaned into her, evidence of his *enjoyment* grazing the inside of her thigh. "Didn't you?"

"Does it matter? It was completely unprofessional. I shouldn't have let it happen. You shouldn't have done it!" She backed away, gnawing at her thumbnail. "Why did you do it?"

"Please tell me that's a rhetorical question."

"You didn't mean it. You're upset, you needed someone to comfort you, and I was here."

"I don't *need* anything, Sara." His eyes frosted over. "Especially pity. If you have to ask why I kissed you, then I obviously made a mistake."

A strangled sound made its way out of her mouth. "It *was* a mistake," she whispered.

"Then maybe now's a good time to walk away. So we don't make any more." Cold, detached, hollow. It was as if any emotion that had come bubbling to the surface receded when she didn't fall back into his waiting arms. He yanked a t-shirt over his head, slipped on two different colored ankle socks, and slid his feet into a pair of sneakers, no longer acknowledging she was even in the room.

"You're exactly what everyone else sees. I can't believe I thought for a minute you might be different." She *was* that pitiful girl, much as she hated to admit it. Caught in his complicated web, believing he might have the capacity to care after all. But he didn't. And he never would. Life was a game to him, and he was on a perpetual quest to win at any cost, never considering there might be collateral damage along the way.

He pulled open the door, pausing long enough to stifle her with a glare that made her blood run cold. "Yeah, well, life is just full of disappointments, isn't it?"

The door slammed, shaking the walls, and shattering her heart like the glass jar in the bathroom.

What had she done?

NINETEEN

"WHY ARE YOU WASTING YOUR TIME with her? She can't give you what you need." Gia's breathy voice made the hairs on the back of his neck stand on end as he stormed into the desolate arena corridor.

Daxton gritted his teeth, his pride as bruised as his shins. "Mind your own business, Gia."

Gia sidled toward him, puffing out her ample chest, her high heels clicking on the concrete. How she was able to breathe with those tits poured into such a tight top was beyond him. She ran her fingertips down his arms, the sensation making his stomach roll. He wanted Sara's hands on him, but she RSVP'd a big fat no to *that* party. *Fuck!* If he didn't know better, he'd have thought he clocked his head on a rock out there in the parking lot. Inside out over a girl who wanted nothing to do with him, and unable to get hard for a chick who couldn't get enough of him. "I know what you need. Let me give it to you. Forget the choir girl." She backed him against the wall, her puckered lips poised to attack. They were deviously determined, and he was teetering on the brink of disgusted. She palmed his cock and... *nothing.*

He swatted her hand away. "Cut it out. I'm not in the mood. I have to get to sound check."

"No, you don't. They just switched the schedule and we're up first. We have plenty of time. I need you, Dax. We're so good together. I love the way your cock feels inside me." She gripped his hand, forcing it under her obscenely short denim skirt. "Don't you feel how wet you make me? You want that. I know you do."

"Gia, stop." He pulled away. The hallway was quiet, but for how long? The last thing he needed was for anyone to see him finger-fucking Gia in public. "It was fun, but now it's over, okay?"

Gia's eyes narrowed. She pushed against his chest with the force of her body weight, sending him stumbling backward. A sharp pain exploded down his leg. Damn, this girl had a lot of pent-up rage. "So, that's it? You decided fucking me isn't worth your time anymore, and now you're *done*? I don't get a say? I just have to accept being kicked to the curb?"

"You knew this was never going to turn into anything serious. We agreed to that before we started. Besides, I told you last time we were done." His eyes darted up and down the hall. Still empty. He needed to get the hell away from

Fatal Attraction and *fast*.

"You're a real fucking piece of work, Daxton. You don't give a shit about anyone but yourself." She pounded her fists on his chest again and hissed at him. "You *idiot*. Don't you have any idea who you're dealing with? Or are you just too pretty to be smart?"

He grabbed her wrists and flipped her around so her back was pinned to the wall. "Let me make this very clear. We're *done*. Stay the fuck away from me, Gia."

Her eyes flashed with a malice that chilled the blood in his veins. "You can't stop what's meant to be, Dax. Remember that."

TWENTY

DAMN HIM FOR LEAVING! HE JUST stalked out of the green room without so much as a backward glance, like the hard, unfeeling jackass he was reputed to be. And here Sara was in his wake, wondering, yet again, if she was doomed to be the girl collecting the jagged pieces of her life after yet another person had shattered it.

She pulled out a piece of grape Bubblicious from her running shorts and popped it into her mouth. It wasn't a Popsicle, but it was her best option. Thank goodness for the tiny zippered pocket. Her supply was dwindling, and she needed that juicy grape flavor like a crackhead searching for a fix. Some people drank; she chewed and popped. Except this time, it couldn't repair the gaping hole in her heart.

"Sara."

She blinked back the tears pooling in her eyes. "Merrick, I'm sorry. I should have called you, but Dax--"

"Stop. I'm not here to argue." He let out a sigh, averting his eyes. "I know I've been acting like a prick toward you."

She furrowed her brow. "Okay, thanks for the acknowledgement."

"Look, that's just who I am, so don't take it personally." He folded his arms.

"Merrick, is this supposed to be an apology? Because I'm missing the part where you actually give a crap."

He snickered. "I don't do apologies. Remember? I'm a prick. I just wanted to let you know I'm going to leave you alone from now on. I'll get the PAs to handle the laundry and packing, okay?"

It was hard not to laugh at the ridiculousness of their exchange, even though she was in the depths of despair at what she'd just lost. "Deal. Thanks."

Merrick shrugged. "You need thick skin. Didn't I tell you that way back in the beginning?"

"Yeah." She forced a smile. "You did. My bad."

"So, we're good." He held up his fist. "Pound it."

"Really?"

"What? They don't do it where you come from in Michigan?"

"Minnesota. And, no, they don't." She tapped his fist with her own. "But I guess there's a first time for everything."

"You're a good kid. Now do me a solid and tell Dax to get off my ass."

As if he'd ever speak to her again. "Sure," she mumbled,

the angst lancing her heart.

Merrick saluted her before walking toward the main arena. "Time for sound check. See you there."

Sara wandered through the maze of corridors, edging past teams of roadies and techs rushing to set up the sound system on stage. It was time to ditch the sweaty clothes and get her head screwed back on before the now dreaded sound check. Bright sunshine assaulted her eyes once she ventured outside. The crowds had dissipated for the moment, but they'd be back, just like cockroaches. Darn it, she still needed to schedule that press conference before Kat had a coronary.

Sara pushed open the door to the bus, shoulders hunched. Her bunk barely qualified as a bedroom; heck, it hardly qualified as a *bed*. At least it boasted some degree of privacy with a dark curtain, so she could crumble like a display of dominoes in peace, free to lament for at least ten minutes before a quick shower preceded her newest challenge – how the hell to loosen the vise-like grip Daxton had on her heart.

Her hand froze as she pulled back the curtain, a strangled sob catching in her throat. A postcard sat atop the stark white bedspread. How ironic that the representation of something so deadly could sit innocently atop something so pure and innocuous. Her fingers closed around the card, throat tightening as she gazed at the glossy picture of Lake Hiawatha, crown jewel of Grand Falls, Minnesota. Her home. Her past. Her *horror*.

The lake looked so still, and so serene in the photo. So different than how she remembered it on that ominous night. *Those* waters were menacing, unforgiving…life-taking. The guilt she'd kept buried bubbled to the surface, threatening to erupt. Her ex-boyfriend Brian never had a chance, all because of her. Trembling fingers turned over the photo. Tears stung her eyes as the postcard fluttered to the floor.

You'll never escape.

Breaths escaped her mouth in short, painful gasps. A loud crash from deep within the belly of the bus sent her stumbling backward. A shooting pain ripped through her neck muscles. Twisting her head was near impossible, but she had to get away. Somebody was out there; somebody who knew, and somebody who wanted to make her pay. She dug her phone out of her pocket, fingers trembling over the keyboard to call…who? Her parents, not that they'd bothered to return any of the desperate messages she'd already left. Jake? Eli? *Daxton?* And in all likelihood, nobody could help her. She was drowning with no lifeboat in sight.

Sara inhaled, a biting scent of marijuana permeating her senses. If she stayed on this bus a second longer, she'd be too baked to move. The air was so polluted with weed, her eyes burned with each panicked step toward the door. The bus was still dark, save for a thin stream of light coming from one of the other bunks. A clear escape path led her to fresh air. Roadies milled about, pushing equipment around the expansive lot. Photographers were perched alongside the tour buses, waiting for any glimpse at the headliners. Her eyes darted in every direction, painfully aware of everything around her, yet completely eluded her at the same time. There was no grim reaper lurking with a sickle. There were just…people. But *people* had put her in her current predicament.

She ran into the arena, pushing past the equipment teams and their huge setups. Heck, for all she knew, she could be running from one of *them*. Her mind was blank, but her legs propelled her toward the main arena stage. Jimmy Sixx was supposed to be in sound check. What a freaking hypocrite she was, wanting to kick Eli to the curb because she didn't need anyone protecting her, and yet here she was, running toward the one person who—

Screams drowned out the rest of the acidic thought. Her heart rate rocketed, beads of perspiration popping up on the back of her neck. She ran faster, her sneakers pounding on the concrete floor. Sean from security pushed past her and jumped onto the stage, the rest of the team in tow. She skidded to a stop in front of the stage, clapping a hand to her mouth to silence the gasp. Gia Lourdes lay still in a crumbled heap, trapped under a huge metal lighting fixture. Good God, that thing must have weighed at least a hundred pounds. Blood poured from the lacerations on Gia's face and arms. Jesus, there was red everywhere.

Sara watched in stunned silence. The girls of Smeared Lipstick were in hysterics, especially Laney. Her words were barely discernible through the sobs. She'd fallen to the ground next to Gia, tears streaming down her face. The beefy security guards heaved the fixture off Gia's limp body, while medics buzzed around, checking her vitals.

"Everybody stay back, please. Give them some room to work on her."

The air was so thick; Sara could barely inhale. *It wasn't*

supposed to be Gia. She had a gut feeling that this *accident* was meant for her. Pain and suffering were meant for *her*. *She* was the one that was supposed to be at the sound check. When had the schedule changed? And why hadn't she been told? Gia's body was lifted onto a gurney and a path was cleared to the exit. *Please let her be alive.*

Hordes of medics, publicists, and band managers flanked all sides of the gurney, rushing to the waiting ambulances, guarding Gia from the relentless photogs camped outside the arena entrance. Sara's feet were rooted to the spot, and even in the middle of a crowd, she felt more alone and afraid than she'd have ever imagined possible. A strong hand pressed onto her shoulder. She yelped, twisting away, only to feel a bandaged palm close around her wrist. Tears clouded her vision. Daxton's familiar scent floated into the air, filling her with relief, security, and hope. She collapsed against his muscular chest, teeth chattering. "You were supposed to be up there. *I* was supposed to be up there. Gia is…she's…oh my God, what if she doesn't make it? This is my fault! It wasn't supposed to be her. I'm so sorry, Dax, I should have never pushed you away, but I'm…I'm so scared."

"Shh." He pulled her against him. How was it possible that his arms alone could provide solace while everything crumbled, including her sanity? "It's going to be okay. They're going to take care of her."

She swiped away the tears. Air blew from the overhead vents, chilling her from the outside in. "You don't know that. She might not make it. It should have been me!" A throbbing sensation between her temples persisted. "I should be lying on that gurney!"

Daxton tilted her chin, concern shadowing his features. "You're not making sense. What does this have to do with you?"

"I can't...please...you need to get away from me. Gia got hurt because of me and I don't want..."

"Dax! What the hell happened? I just saw the ambulances take off. Coop, Liam, and Finn followed them to the hospital. Don't you think you should have gone, too?" Merrick nodded toward Sara. "I'm sure your publicist would agree."

"Fuck off, Merrick. She's upset. And yes, I *am* going to the hospital."

"Good. It's the right thing to do, considering you've been nailing Gia every third day since this tour started."

Sara flinched at Merrick's acidic tone. Why was he looking at her like that? What about that fist-pounding crap? Just when she thought things between them were trending toward civil, too. Did he get pleasure out of yanking her heart out of her chest, spitting on it, then clubbing it until it was flatter than a pancake with no hope of ever regaining shape or function? Did she really need to hear the sordid details? Even though deep down, she'd known this was the life Daxton had chosen, regardless of what he claimed otherwise.

Daxton's arms dropped from her waist. Coldness snaked through her insides, as if her body sensed his lack of presence, craving any reassuring touch, confirming she wasn't alone, exposed and vulnerable. She hugged her arms tightly around her own waist, stray hairs blowing around her tear-streaked face.

"Don't fucking talk to me like that. And there's no need to be so crude in front of Sara." His voice was low and menacing, the tone alone making Merrick stumble backward.

Merrick's eyes narrowed, dark as the ace of spades in the dim lighting. "You'd better watch yourself, Dax. I won't hesitate to knock you on your fucking ass."

Daxton inched closer to him, fists clenched. "Leave. *Now*."

Merrick's face twisted into an evil grimace. "Just get to the hospital," he muttered before turning on his heel and storming toward the exit.

Daxton grabbed her hand, leading her out of the arena. The crowds had dispersed, and the corridors were near empty, save for a few cops gathering reports on the accident from the equipment teams. He stopped short and twisted toward her, his fingertips caressing the side of her face, swiping at the tears that fell. "Sara, about what Merrick said..."

"Can we please just go?" She shivered against him. "I don't want to be here right now."

"Yeah, of course." He grasped her hand, leading her through the maze of hallways toward a blocked off exit. Her eyes darted in all directions as Daxton spoke to the head of security. Nobody had followed, and nobody was coming for her...*yet*.

TWENTY-ONE

DAXTON PULLED OPEN THE DOOR OF the tour bus and guided Sara up the steps. They'd managed to avoid the press on their way out, since everyone with a camera was fixated on what had happened inside the arena and who had been loaded into the ambulance. The guys were all at the hospital, leaving them alone on the bus for the foreseeable future. He closed the door to his bedroom and flipped the lock. With a slow turn, he pulled Sara tight into his arms. "Okay, you're safe now. Tell me what's going on. Why are you so freaked out? Why should it have been you?"

"Daxton, please. I can't tell you. It's bad. God, it's so bad, and I thought I could escape. I figured they'd never find me here, but I was wrong. And now, Gia—"

"Shhh. Take it easy. Sit down for a minute." He walked

130

over to the bar, poured an amber-colored liquor into a glass, and then handed it to her. "Drink this."

"Thank you." Her hand trembled as she raised the cool crystal to her lips. At least her teeth had stopped chattering for a few seconds, allowing her to gulp the liquid.

Daxton watched as her shoulders stopped quaking. "Sara, I didn't want you to find out about Gia that way. Merrick is an insensitive asshole. It didn't mean anything, and I never meant to hurt you. I thought you were still with Eli and I…I just couldn't handle being around you. You were all I thought about."

Sara hugged herself, her body still visibly shaking. "Dax, it's fine. I understand. I'm not mad, and you don't owe me any explanations. Whatever happened between you guys was your business. And I did have Eli. It's just that…" She took a deep breath. "…from the moment we met, I haven't been able to think about anyone *but* you. I should have ended things with Eli a long time ago. My heart has been telling me to run to you for a while. I was just too stubborn to listen. But I am listening now." She gnawed her lower lip, studying her hands.

"It's about damn time." The corners of Daxton's lips curled upward. He caressed the sides of her face, the pained expression visibly calming under his touch. "How about we forget the past? I only care about what happens next, as long as it involves you."

"That's the problem, Dax; *my* past won't let me forget. I can't escape it." The fear was back, washing over her features. "There was an accident. A guy I was dating back home…Brian…he was bad news, mixed up with drugs, dropped out of school, couldn't hold a job. My parents never cared about me, only about their image. My dad's the mayor, so appearances are everything. I got tired of being the trophy daughter and started sneaking around with this guy. One night, we were at a party on the lake. He'd gotten pretty trashed and we fought. He accused me of cheating on him. I tried to convince him it wasn't true, but he was high and irate. He shoved me onto a boat and rowed us to the middle. It was so dark, and everyone had left by then. No amount of screaming would have helped me. He tried...he tried to rape me. We struggled, and I grabbed an oar and swung it as hard as I could, knocking him out of the boat." Tears pooled in her eyes, her voice trembling. "He couldn't swim. I didn't know that, and I...I..."

Daxton wrapped his arms around her, stroking the small of her back. "It's okay."

She pulled away, swiping at the tears now streaming down her face. "No. I let him drown. I didn't help him. It's my fault he died."

"You were in shock, trying to protect yourself. Didn't you tell your story to the cops?"

"No, the police only know that it was a drowning accident. I lied and told them he was goofing around and fell out of the boat. That's it. Not that he was wasted and tried to rape me because I told him it was over between us," she whispered. "That's why I left. My parents sent me away, telling everyone that I was too traumatized by the accident, when in reality, they sent me away because of what it could do to my dad's career. He was in the middle of re-election. If his daughter had been brought up on murder charges..."

She shook her head. "It wouldn't have mattered if it were self-defense or not. And now, I've been getting threats. Somebody knows what really happened, and they've found me. I thought I could escape, but it's too late. Gia's in the hospital. That wasn't an accident. It was supposed to be me, not her!"

"Sara, you didn't do anything wrong. It was self-defense. You did what you had to do."

"I still should have saved him."

"Why? So he could have killed you?" He cupped her chin. "You had to protect yourself."

"Somebody is threatening me, Dax. I don't know who, or how they know, but they want me to suffer. I don't know what to do."

"Nobody is going to hurt you. I promise I won't let anything happen to you. And what happened to Gia was an accident. You don't know that it was meant for you." His thumb wiped away a tear. "But just in case, I'll take care of security. You'll be safe."

"You know, you're the only person who makes me feel that way." She bit her lower lip. God, he wanted her with every fiber of his being. He was desperate to stroke her hair, to drag his fingertips down the slope of her back, and to feel her body pressed against his. The emotion in her gaze morphed into something very different in that instant…need, lust, desire…or some combination of the three. "I'm sorry about before. I shouldn't have let you leave like that. That kiss wasn't a mistake. It was incredible, and I just…"

Dizzy. So much so, he could barely think. His body had taken over, commanding his every movement - hands acting of their own accord were now lost in her thick blonde hair, lips crushing against her grape-flavored ones. Pipe dreams were overrated. He needed this...*her*...even if it were the only opportunity he got before they both acknowledged none of this was real, or that the tour was some kind of alternate reality where life was lived within a self-indulgent bubble. Screw it; he'd deal with that another time. Now wasn't the time to obsess, not when they'd finally given in to the fantasy. A delicious ache had settled in his groin, one that only she could ease. Her mouth was so hot against his own - determined, insistent, and hungry. She drank him in like a plant in need of water and sunshine and dammit, he wanted that mouth on so many other places.

He slid off her jacket, grazing the soft skin of her shoulders, as his lips trailed the smooth column of her neck. The scent of spun sugar hit his nostrils, so sweet and pure. She melted against him, arching her back, making the tight t-shirt stretch against her pert breasts.

Rock solid. She hadn't even laid a finger on him and his cock throbbed, straining against his jeans, ready to erupt like Mount Saint Helens. Firm thighs straddled him. Blood rushed to his cock, the ache intensifying with each hip roll. The globes of her ass were so perfect – tight and smooth. He grasped them, squeezing a mewl out of her before his hands slipped into her shorts and skated over soft, flimsy lace that barely covered places he longed to taste and touch. She was wet, so fucking wet for him. The thought of driving himself into her heat could make him blow like a teenaged boy jerking off for the first time.

Her fingers fumbled with the buttons on his jeans.

He was dying a slow death from the torture of restraint. Dammit, he'd burn every single pair of those button-flies later. Seconds felt like hours, until she'd freed him from the confines of fabric. But, oh God, it was worth the wait. A few pumps of her hand and he was ready to combust. The head of his cock rubbed against her soaked panties. They were drenched because she was every bit as hot for him as he was for her. *Fuck, yeah.*

He slid his fingers under the lace, plunging into her slick opening. It was so soft and warm, the walls quivering as he stroked her clit before delving back into her core, over and over. A soft sigh escaped her swollen lips, so juicy and bitable. A tingling sensation deep within his balls was enough of a warning. He was hovering on the brink, and dammit, he wanted her to fall over the edge right alongside him.

With one swift movement, he had Sara on her back, resting on the plush red comforter. Her cheeks were flushed, her hair was mussed, and her porcelain complexion was a stark contrast to the vibrant color surrounding her. She was so beautiful, vulnerable, and...*real*. She lifted her arms, a smile playing with the corners of her mouth. "Don't stop now, you're on a roll."

His cock twitched, still stiff, still aching with need. He pulled off her shirt and tossed it aside. Her breasts, plump and heaving, were squeezed into a black sports bra. With the flick of his fingers, they were free - perfect, lush, and all for him. Her deep pink nipples were taut, begging to be teased, and he was all too willing to comply. But he wanted, no, *needed*, so much more...everything she had to give.

His tongue traced a path to her navel, halting at the waistband of her shorts. Knowing what waited for him beneath the layers of clothing was maddening, and he couldn't yank them off fast enough. The shorts and panties dropped to the floor, allowing her creamy thighs to fall open, inviting and taunting him at the same time. Every nip, lick, and suckle made her writhe against his greedy mouth, mewls fast becoming pleas for more. Tearing himself away was pure agony, but knowing he would soon be buried deep within her was the only consolation. And fuck him if he couldn't wait one more second.

He yanked open his shirt, buttons popping through the air. His jeans pooled around his ankles until he kicked them across the room.

Sara sat back on her elbows, a teasing smile on her face, her green eyes dark with lust. "How much longer are you going to make me wait?"

He crawled onto the bed, shifting her onto his lap. "Depends. How much do you want it?"

Her skin was so soft, plastered against his. The head of his cock grazed her opening. With one arm still holding her in place, he grabbed a condom from the drawer, bit open the package, and rolled it on. *Tricks of the trade. Can't always have use of both arms. Gotta improvise.*

He knelt in front of her and pulled her legs around his waist, gathering her in his arms. Warmth encased him as she slid onto his aching shaft, her walls clenching around him. Heat emanated from her core with each thrust, suffocating him with a seemingly insatiable craving. Her body pulled him deeper into the abyss where he was drowning in all that she was, no lifeboat in sight, and no desire to be rescued.

Their bodies rocked together, slick with sweat, unwilling to part. He eased her back onto the comforter, his length pulsating deep within her center, each intense movement powered by all the unresolved emotions coursing through him. This girl, their unlikely connection, his heart…everything that had made sense before was now in upheaval. And he didn't know if he ever wanted things to be set right again.

He lowered his head, staring into those vibrant eyes before pressing his lips to hers, needing that final connection before they tumbled over the edge and into the unknown. The coiling heat of her tongue swirled around his own, sending shudders rippling through his body. There was no such thing as being too close. With Sara, he could never be immersed enough to feel completely sated. Her muscles clenched and squeezed until tiny sparks deep within his core ignited, a slow explosion rumbling, gathering force until the blast shot into his extremities. Every nerve ending fired at once, toe-curling sensations tearing through his limbs, singeing everything in their wake. He wanted to scream, laugh, and cry at the same time, never having been touched at this level by another. Swells of pleasure crashed over him, while white light blinded him, overtaking all rational thought. Hell, his mind was such an empty canvas, he might have even blacked out from the intensity. Un-fucking-believable.

He collapsed onto his elbows, hovering over her heaving body. "You're still conscious. I didn't do my job."

"Clearly not." She let out an exaggerated sigh and rolled her eyes. "Disappointing. I expected more."

"Can I get another shot?" He smoothed a damp strand of hair away from her face. "I'll do better next time."

"I don't know. What if you expended all your energy *running* this morning?"

"Screw cardio. I'd rather find other ways to exercise."

"I can definitely think of some creative ways to get your heart pumping." She tightened her arms around his waist.

His lips brushed against her forehead. "I want to try every single one. We won't leave any stone unturned. All in the name of health and wellness."

Her smile faded. The expression, which had been happy and relaxed only seconds earlier, was again clouded by fear. "Later. You need to go to the hospital. And I need to deal with the press."

"After a quick nap. Hey," he murmured against her ear. "I'm not leaving you, okay? We'll take care of this together. Don't be scared."

"Promise?"

"Yeah." Because being without her just wasn't an option. Not anymore.

TWENTY-TWO

A BLARING NOISE PUNCTURED SUCH A delicious dream; the one where Daxton stripped her down to her most vulnerable, and rocketed her body to another galaxy with his massive—

Strong arms tightened around her, a warm breath fluttering against her neck like feathers. She bit her lip and released a deep sigh. Daxton pulled her closer. Sweet Jesus, it had been real. She didn't think those sensations were even possible outside of a dream sequence.

"Are you going to answer your phone?"

"If I don't, it'll just keep ringing."

His lips nuzzled her ear. "Ignore it. I like taking midday naps with you."

"But if we don't get up now, we'll never sleep tonight."

"That's a problem I'd really like to have."

She giggled and grabbed her phone. "Seriously, though. You need to get to the hospital, and I need to call my boss Jake before I get fired."

"Correction, you are coming to the hospital with me, and you can call Jake on the way."

Sara flipped over. His hair was mussed, flopping over his half-hooded eyes. His lips curled into a wicked smirk. "Unless you decide to stay right here and let me do very bad things to you. That would be my vote."

She wrapped her arms around his waist, running her fingers down his muscular back. He smelled so good. Jeez, what kind of soap did this guy use? Whatever the scent was, she needed it bottled. Like, yesterday.

"You know we can't stay in here forever. There's so much to do. I need to put a press release together, contact all the local and national media outlets, arrange a press conference…"

"Don't worry about it. And that's not all your job. Your only job is worrying about me, remember? The other crap is what managers are for. Let Merrick and Eli take care of everything else."

Warm lips brushed hers, the mere taste of him igniting her desire as if she hadn't just been catapulted into the land of Ecstasy only an hour earlier. Every cell in her body was alive and awake, craving everything and anything Daxton had to offer.

The iPhone pinged again. A deep sigh deflated her body. "Come on. The faster we handle everything, the quicker we can get back here." With a quick peck on the cheek, she crawled toward the edge of the bed and grabbed her clothes.

"Okay, fine. We'll do it your way. Just get dressed really slowly...don't rush it. Maybe play with your—"

She rolled her eyes. "You're not helping at all."

He swung his legs over the side and grabbed his boxer-briefs and jeans. Watching out of the corner of her eye, she contemplated taking just a few more minutes to...No! Yes, she wanted to trace every single inch of his abs with her tongue, but it had to wait. Too much had happened, and plenty more needed to be fixed.

Daxton pulled a Ramones t-shirt over his head and grabbed his Houston Astros baseball cap. He fished around a drawer and pulled out two different socks – one was white with a black Nike swish, and the other was bright red.

God, he looked so scrumptious in that cap. "Can I ask you something?"

"On or off the record?"

She smiled. "Cute. Now tell me, what's the deal with your socks?"

"What do you mean?"

"They never match. Why is that?"

He sank onto the bed and yanked on the socks, a faraway look in his eyes. "Growing up, my mom did the laundry for Jase and me, and one sock out of every pair would always get lost in the shuffle. The strays would show up later, on a towel or stuck in a shirt. It became a big joke. We'd end up wearing each other's socks, and we were always mismatched. It was our thing. So now, I always wear two different ones. The match will always be Jase's."

"That's really sweet."

A small smile lifted his lips. "Ready?"

She nodded, her heart thrumming harder with each step he took toward her. "Yes, but I need to grab a few things from my bus." She dangled one piece of a lace thong. "Someone ripped my favorite panties."

When his sinful lips pressed against hers, it all but exploded in her chest. Heat swirled in her core, radiating from her body, every square inch of her skin screaming for those lips to singe the surface.

Oh God, yes. She was ready, but not for what would greet her outside that tour bus.

TWENTY-THREE

T HOSE DAMNED CABLES. SNAPPING TOO early and fucking up the plan. It should have been a game of double jeopardy, except one of the targets had been missing. Eh. At least one of them was out of the limelight.

Death wasn't the objective, at least not for Gia. Just pain; enough that she'd be out of commission for the rest of the tour. A broken leg, a fractured arm. Whatever would keep her away from her beloved drums and off Daxton's cock.

Who the hell knew she'd be directly underneath the fixture? One of those dumbass stage managers must have adjusted the stage schematics, and she ended up taking the full impact, ending up with a crushed pelvis, shattered spine, and massive concussion. Not the intent, but hey, there's always potential for collateral damage.

And Sara? The victim who'd somehow managed to escape her fate?

Just thinking the name conjured up stomach-twisting images of her and Daxton, no doubt wrapped in each other's arms on that tour bus - writhing, sweating, panting...

A deep breath did little to calm the brewing storm. Sara was indeed reliably unreliable. But that would only protect her for so long.

TWENTY-FOUR

"**S**ARA! WHERE THE HELL HAVE YOU been? I just spoke to Jake. He needs you to handle the logistics for the press conference asap." Kat tapped her fingernails against the cinderblock wall in the arena corridor. "This is a total disaster, and I can't be babysitting you while I'm trying to do damage control for this tour."

"Kat, relax. She was with me. We were working on a statement."

Kat smirked. "*Really*, Dax. A statement. And what did you come up with? Anything PG I can use on Twitter?"

Daxton snickered. "It needs more work. Listen, Sara stays with me. Whatever you need, say the word, but we're a package deal, okay?"

Kat shrugged. "Fine. Sara, here are the lists of to-dos

from the office in Houston."

Sara reached out and grabbed the papers from Kat. "Don't worry, I will take care of everything. I'm on my way to the pressroom now. Have you confirmed the new opening band?"

"Yes, I got word that Punk'd is all lined up and ready to fly out here. We'll need to cancel tonight's show. I've updated all of the online news outlets and our accounts. Jake has everyone on deck back in Houston to handle inquiries, and I'll handle the social media updates and buzz from here. Jake will forward the riders for Punk'd soon, and they need to be given to the PAs." Kat pointed at the stack of papers now in Sara's hands. "First things first, let's get the press conference scheduled. Shoot for seven o'clock."

"Yes." Sara nodded. Her eyes flickered over to Daxton's. "I have to make some calls. Can I use your green room?"

"Yeah, I'll come with you."

Kat rolled her eyes. "Dax, get to the hospital. You're already calling too much attention to yourself by not being with the rest of the band. Sara, give me a holler if you have any questions." She spun on her insanely high heels and stalked down the hallway.

Sara's mouth fell open. "Holy cow, I'm so getting fired."

"You're not getting fired. We can handle all of this." His blaring iPhone ring echoed in the concrete expanse. "Yeah?"

"Dax, it's Sean. I have the guy from last night."

"What do you mean, you have him?"

"He's in the security shed. Said he needs to talk to you." Sean's voice dropped, almost muffled. "He's got something,

Dax. Something you need to see."

"I don't care what he has."

"Trust me, you do."

Whoever this clown was, whatever he wanted, he'd reached the end of the line. His mother was gone, and nothing this guy could say would erase all the pain she'd caused. He let out a shaky breath, wiping his clammy palms against his jeans. Lying to himself, pretending not to care, and bottling up all those useless emotions never gave him the closure he so desperately needed. Maybe he'd never get it. His eyes flickered to Sara's concerned gaze. But could he really be whole again, or love again, without letting go of the anger? This toxic existence he'd been living was so empty, cold, and lonely. He didn't want that life anymore. He wanted Sara. He had to try for her; otherwise, the noose around his neck would eventually suffocate him.

"I'll meet you both in the green room." Daxton clicked off the phone, his gaze unwavering.

"What is it?" She bit her lower lip, her face masked with alarm. "Is everything okay?"

He grasped her hand. "Everything is going to be fine." Those words were such bullshit. Would they ever have real meaning behind them? Would anything ever truly be 'okay'?

Each step closer to the green room made the lump in his throat grow larger and larger. By the time they'd made it to the doorway, it was a miracle he could still swallow.

"I can't feel my fingers anymore," she murmured.

He loosened his grip on her hand. "Sorry."

"Tell me, Dax." She knew something was up. She could

tell. Always. How was it possible she could see him so clear-ly when nobody else could? Was it because nobody else cared to see anything beyond the surface? That it was easier to accept him at face value, rather than understand what made him this way?

"The guy from last night. He's back."

"So just let security handle—"

"No. I need to talk to him, to face whatever it is he has to say. There's some link to my mom and I just…" He pushed back his hair. "…I can't carry this with me anymore, Sara. I have to lay it to rest; otherwise, I won't be able to move forward. And I want to, so badly."

"I don't understand…lay what to rest?"

"The bitterness, the resentment, the anger. It's killing me, and I'm not ready to die. I didn't care before – who I hurt, who I screwed, who I got high with…none of it mat-tered." He tilted her chin toward him. "It does now."

Tears gathered in her green eyes, the ones he wanted to lose himself in forever. Drowning in those pools was the only place where he'd be able to breathe, to survive. A sin-gle one escaped, trailing down her flushed cheek until his thumb wiped it away. "I finally know what matters, and I'm not about to mess it up."

He turned the doorknob, pushing open the door. Sean stood in front of the couch, his beefy arms folded, a men-acing look on his face. The look disappeared when he saw Dax. "I've checked him out and he's clean. You want me to stay?"

"No, but I need you guys to take Sara to the pressroom, okay? Don't leave her side." Daxton turned to Sara. "I'll be there soon."

"Okay." She leaned closer, up on her tiptoes, before her soft lips brushed against his cheek. "I'll be waiting."

Sean followed Sara out of the room and pulled the door closed. Dax leaned against it, eyeing the man in front of him. He was jittery, unable to even sit back on the cushion.

"Who are you and why are you here?" No sense beating around the bush. He was on a quest for closure and this guy held the key. Or so he claimed.

"I'll answer your questions, but you should see something first." The man pulled out a letter and a small jewelry box. "My name is Sam. I did know your mother, and she wanted you to have these. Begged me to bring them to you."

"Where is she?"

Sam wrung his hands together and held his head. "She's gone. Passed away a few weeks ago."

The words hit him like a cement block to the chest. So many questions assaulted his mind, but his lips refused to form sentences. Daxton sank onto the couch across from Sam. The wound he'd been haphazardly nursing every day since his mother had left was torn open, leaving him raw, exposed, and *devastated*. By a stranger. Fuck, it hurt, worse than any pain he'd ever experienced. His fingers closed around the letter. Sam looked up and Daxton saw everything he felt in his heart reflected in this man's tortured gaze – regret, sadness, loss.

"Read the letter, Daxton."

It was dated two months ago. The words, written in his mother's familiar script, exploded like bullets in his brain. Phrases swam in front of his watery eyes, his mind trying

149

to process everything on the page.

...cancer...death...Jase...father...Sam...love... goodbye...

He crumbled the paper into a tight ball and hurled it against the wall. "Why the fuck are you here?"

Sam recoiled. "Dax, I'm here because your mom wanted you to know the truth."

Rage that had bubbled just below the surface for the past year poured out of him like lava from an erupting volcano. He grabbed an empty highball glass and flung it against the wall, the shattering sound mimicking the feeling in his chest. "The *truth*? That my own biological father couldn't give a shit less about me and was willing to take a payoff from Tyler before walking away with your dick tucked between your legs? That you didn't give a flying fuck about me enough to find me before all this happened? That you didn't give a fuck about me at *all*? Because that's what I got out of the letter!" His heart thundered against his ribcage, beads of perspiration popping up along the back of his neck. His breaths grew shallow and harsh, the air piercing his lungs like sharp knives. "She left me, her own son! I loved her more than anything. I would have taken care of her. But she ran back to you." He inched closer, voice shaking. "To you, the worthless piece of shit who abandoned his son."

"Dax, I never meant to hurt you. Please believe me. I loved your mother, but I knew I couldn't offer her the life she deserved. I left both of you so that you'd be taken care of. I never cashed that check. I didn't want Tyler's money. I just wanted you to have the best life possible. That's why

I left."

"Do you want some kind of medal for not taking that money? Should I pat you on the back, *Dad*?" He paced the room, ignoring his ringing phone. "You're a selfish asshole. A real man wouldn't walk away from his responsibility as a parent, and certainly wouldn't leave his own kid to be raised by someone else."

"You're right. It was wrong of me to discard you like that. But Tyler made it clear—"

"Fuck Tyler!" Daxton flipped over a table, liquor bottles crashing to the floor. "You let him call the shots? You're fucking weak! A pathetic excuse for a man…for a fucking human being!"

"Dax, please. I came to try and fix this. Just give me a chance. I realize what I lost all those years ago. Your mother's death crushed me, and I regret every day I didn't have her in my life. I wasted so much time. I don't want to lose any more."

Daxton gripped the top of the couch, his thoughts swallowed by the clanging between his ears. Clenching the leather in his fists was the only way to keep them from pummeling Sam. "You're twenty-four years too late. Thank you for showing me the kind of man I never want to become."

"Dax, give me a chance. I'm your father. I want to make things right."

"You're not my father. You were a sperm donor, nothing more." He opened the door. "Thanks, you've delivered your message. Now you can get the fuck out."

Sam rose from the couch, eye-level with Dax. Same dark hair, same deep-set eyes, same muscular build. But beneath the surface, Sam represented everything Dax resisted. For all these years, he'd felt out of place, unwanted, and rootless. But standing next to this man, his legitimate father, it only amplified the feelings of rejection and abandonment. Through the years, Tyler had been cold, unfeeling, and standoffish. And even though he took care of Daxton as if he were his biological son, their relationship was rocky at best. They'd spent more time at odds than not, but Tyler never walked away from his self-imposed responsibilities. Not even when his mother left.

Now she was gone forever, and he'd never be able to talk to her again. He'd never be able to tell her how much he'd missed her, to cry at her bedside, or to say goodbye. He'd been grieving the loss for so long, yet the emptiness always remained, along with the flicker of hope that she'd come back. Damn her for thinking she knew best and for breaking his heart.

Closure. It had always eluded him. Maybe it was because he was on a never-ending futile quest – always trying to tie up the wrong ends…for the wrong reasons.

TWENTY-FIVE

MICS WERE ALL IN PLACE AND TESTED, and the room was set up according to the specifications she'd received from her boss. Calls to all the local press outlets were in progress, and Sara's phone beeped incessantly with notifications from the team in Houston. But what would the message be? She'd been so occupied with the press conference, Gia's condition eluded her, though all accounts were dismal. She seemed like such a sweet girl, always so peppy, and talented as hell. *It shouldn't have been her. It should have been me.*

Her ringtone echoed in the empty room, silencing the dark thoughts. Casie's name flashed on the screen. She stabbed the Accept button. "Casie, have you heard anything? How's Gia?"

"Still in surgery. She's in bad shape. They induced a

coma to bring down the swelling in her brain, but her body is really mangled. It doesn't look good. Lots of internal bleeding, too. That's the big concern right now."

"Oh my God…is she going to…?" *No, don't even say it.* If Sara had been on that stage minutes earlier as planned, she'd have been lying on that gurney alongside Gia.

Casie sighed. "I really don't know. Just try and hold it together. We're handling the situation here at home. Stick with Kat; make sure she has your support and run point on anything she needs. We'll get everything taken care of, I promise."

"Okay."

"Just remember, nobody makes a comment until after the press conference."

"Got it." Sara's throat tightened.

"Security is ramping up as we speak. I've made arrangements for local police to monitor stage setup crews for the remainder of the tour to make sure there's no foul play. No stones will be left unturned."

Sara tugged at her earring. Daxton had spoken to security about her situation. They must have alerted the police. Better to let the authorities handle the investigation and for her to keep quiet. If something leaked, it might put the whole tour in jeopardy. It was time to trust in the team paid very highly for their protective services. "Let me know if you hear anything else."

"Hang in there. We'll chat again later." *Click.*

Sara gnawed at her lip and studied the pages of notes in her hand, full of details about Punk'd, the replacement opening band – three guys, kind of dirt baggy-looking, greasy, and tattooed. Maybe the appeal was in their music. Riders for each scheduled venue for the remainder of the tour had been faxed over, and the PAs needed to start gathering items for the green rooms.

Green rooms…Dax. Where was he? He said he'd be back as soon as—

Another loud ring sent her leaping into the air with a gasp. Jeez, she was so jittery. Guess that was an unfortunate consequence of being stalked by a psychopath.

Her throat tightened as she stabbed the Accept button for the second time. "Mom?"

"Sara, what is so urgent? Don't you know it's election season? Your father and I have been working night and day on the campaign. You're supposed to be keeping yourself occupied and out of trouble with that little public relations job in Houston."

"I'm not in Houston right now. I'm in Phoenix, on tour with a band. There's been an accident." Her voice quivered. "I've been getting threats, Mom. Someone knows about that night."

"Sara, I really don't have time to play a role in your soap opera. You've already done plenty to sabotage your father's career. I don't think I need to remind you that had you been a better, more obedient daughter, you never would have gotten yourself into this predicament in the first place. Our lives have been thrown into upheaval because of your poor judgment."

Tears stung her eyes. "Why is it always about you? Do you even care that someone is after me and trying to hurt me?"

"Enough with the dramatics. We have tried for so long to steer you in the right direction, but all you did was rebel and challenge us at every turn. Your behavior was appalling – parading around with your delinquent *boyfriends*, the drinking, the drugs...frankly, I'm glad you're gone. Shame on me, I thought we'd raised you better."

"Shame on you is right! You've treated me like an accessory all my life! I was a prop, not a daughter! Color-coordinated, coiffed, and manicured. Smile when I say. Retreat to your room when we're done with the photo-ops. Speak only when spoken to. Keep the pole up your ass. It'll help with your posture."

"We gave you everything and you pissed it all away. You left because you weren't strong enough to face the situation *you* created!"

"That's not true! You and Dad banished me so it wouldn't hurt your perfect little bullshit life!" The anger she'd kept bottled up for the past twenty-two years erupted, and the release wasn't nearly as cathartic as she'd hoped. Because at the end of the day, her worst fears had been confirmed. Beneath all the posturing, her parents really didn't care at all. She was a component of their plans, a checkmark on the list of requirements for a political candidate. There was no remorse or tearful apology from her mother.

Cold was an understatement for the tone of her mother's voice. It was more like top-of-Mount-Everest-frigid. "If that's how you really feel, Sara, then I think we're done. Your father and I have spent far too long trying to clean up the messes you've created."

"You know what, Mom? Maybe if you'd treated me

like a daughter instead of an employee, things between us might be different. I know I've made a lot of mistakes, and I have a list of regrets miles long. But isn't the point of living and learning that you try to make your situation better? To reconcile with the people you've wronged?"

The silence was devastating, and so telling at the same time. "I can't discuss this anymore. Your father needs me."

Sara's heart plummeted into her designer boots as the line went dead. *Your father needs me.* What about your daughter? Doesn't she rate? Did she ever?

She stared at the phone in her hand, the answer plain as day. With a stifled sob, she sank into one of the chairs. Her life had been a gargantuan snowball of mistakes and regrets, gathering speed, poised to crush her.

"I'm sorry!" Tears came, fast and furious, streaming down her face, washing away all remnants of the person she was covering up. The makeup, the clothes, the shoes… the façade finally crumbled, revealing what had been broken for so long. "God, I'm so sorry!" Would she ever get the chance to be whole again, to prevent the past from consuming every remaining shred of happiness in her life? Or was she destined to suffer alone, punishment for the ills inflicted at her hand? She clenched her fists, expelling a long, steady breath. No, this was a new chapter, written by *her.* The control she'd always craved, now tightly gripped by her hands, was impossible for anybody to steal. Her story was far from over. It was just beginning.

The door creaked open, and Sean appeared in the doorway, a concerned look on his face. "Sara, what's wrong? Are you okay?"

"Yeah, Sean, life just sucks sometimes, but I'll be fine." Her fate wasn't carved in stone, and dammit, she'd fight like a hellcat to make those words a reality.

TWENTY-SIX

COPS SWARMED THE ACCIDENT SCENE. Teams of engineers and stagehands were still cleaning up the rubble, testing each pulley and cable to figure out how hundreds of pounds of metal fell from the rafters and crushed Gia Lourdes.

Gia's in bad shape. You need to get over here now.

It was the third text from Finn that Daxton had received in the past hour. Of course, the rest of the guys had texted him about twenty more times with similar messages. And there was still a phone call he needed to make to Tyler, but that one had to wait. Anger bubbled in his veins. All this time had passed, and Tyler never said a goddamned word about any of it. His throat tightened, the urge to pick up a bottle of Jack and hurl it against a wall was so overpowering. A temporary fix. Just like everything else in

159

his life. Except Sara. Her presence alone blunted the pain, made him want to resist the fury before it unleashed.

Daxton bolted toward the pressroom. The door was wide open, but where the hell was Sean? Why wasn't he guarding the place? His heart hammered harder with each step until Sara's blonde head appeared. A small smile lifted her quivering lips, her face streaked with tears. She fell into his arms, her shoulders quaking. A strand of hair escaped her messy bun, tickling the stubble on his chin. He smoothed it back, using it as an excuse to trace his fingertips across her soft cheek. "What's wrong, baby? Why are you so upset?"

Her eyes darkened for a fleeting second. "My mom finally called me back."

"What did she say?"

Sara took a deep breath. "Exactly what I thought. She pretty much confirmed I'm on my own. But it's fine. *I'm* fine."

"Are you kidding me? She blew it off?"

"I'm accountable for my decisions, Dax, nobody else."

"So your parents are just going to sit back and watch you be tormented by some psychopath stalker?" What the fuck was wrong with those people? Their daughter's safety was at risk, and they didn't give a good goddamn about it? He clenched his fists, trying to fight the urge to punch a hole in something. Christ, what he'd give to be standing in front of Sara's father right about then.

"Hey. I'm a big girl. I can handle this myself. I made mistakes, and I need to face them, whatever the consequences." She leaned in, nuzzling his ear. "Now go to the hospital. The sooner you go, the sooner you can take me back to bed."

"Much as I like the sound of the last part, there's no way I'm leaving you. You have no idea who you're dealing with."

"I'll be fine. Sean and Kat are here." She pulled away, a determined look on her face. Fierce. Strong. No longer the naïve, scared girl on the run. "Go. Really. Don't let any more time pass."

Another text vibrated his phone. Perfect timing. A quick glance confirmed it was Merrick.

He looked up. "I think you staying here is a really stupid idea."

"Well, that just shows how little faith you have in me."

"It's actually my lack of faith in everyone else."

Her lips brushed against his, making his cock spring to life in immediate response. He swallowed a groan. "Are you sure I can't convince you to come?"

"Save it for later." That wicked gleam in her eye sent blood rushing to his groin.

"You'd better take care of yourself while I'm gone," he grumbled. "You've already teased me too much."

"Just wait until tonight."

Sean walked into the pressroom with a phone pressed to his ear. "Sara, Kat wants to review the attendee list with you and we have to confirm their access to the conference. Nobody gets in without a pass, no exceptions, per the home office in Houston."

"Sure." She nudged Dax. "Go. You have to be back here for the conference in a couple of hours."

"Sean, I'm going to the hospital. Don't leave her side,

okay?" His gaze never strayed from Sara's face. It was almost as if he needed to commit every detail to memory. The strength in her eyes, the resolve in her voice...he'd always sensed there were so many layers to this girl. She wanted her life, her way. Who the hell was he to challenge that?

"You got it, Dax." Sean nodded toward Sara. "I told Kat we'd meet her back in the security shed."

With a final wave, Sara disappeared around a corner with Sean.

Dax pulled out his phone and shot off a quick text to Merrick letting him know he was on his way. He jogged toward the exit and jumped into a waiting SUV, blacked out from top to bottom.

The driver slid into the front seat after slamming the back door shut. "We'll be there in about twenty minutes, Mr. Cole."

"Thanks." He let out a deep breath and skimmed headlines on his phone until they pulled up to the Emergency Room at Banner University Medical Center. All the media outlets were speculating about Gia's condition - nothing positive. A twinge of guilt pricked him. Their last heated exchange, the final break after months of being on-again, off-again...he hadn't mentioned it to anyone. Chick was definitely off her nut, but she was still his friend, and he was an asshole for not going to the hospital sooner. A cold feeling snaked through his insides. Add it to his ever-growing list of regrets.

The driver opened the door and Dax slid on his sunglasses, shielding him from the cameras. The sidewalk outside the entrance was flooded with paparazzi in preparation for his long awaited arrival.

"Daxton, any word on Gia?"

"Is Gia going to make it?"

"They're talking long-term brain damage and paralysis. Can you confirm?"

"Are you two still dating?"

He pushed through the crowd, not uttering a syllable. Fucking vultures. Once inside, Finn grabbed his arm and led him down a hallway.

"She's finally out of surgery. What the fuck took you so long, man?"

"Is she okay?"

"They were able to repair most of the damage to her spine and stop the bleeding, but she's still in a coma and her legs have more pins than a bowling alley."

"Fuck." Dax rubbed a hand down his face.

"Dax, what the hell is going on with you?"

"It's Sara."

Finn furrowed his brow. "What about her?"

"I slept with her."

"Yeah, and?"

"You knew?"

"Did you think we were all on another planet last night when you brought her back to the bus?" Finn snickered. "Well, okay, some of us were."

"But not you."

"Not me. It wasn't really a shocker. You've been cozying up to her since she showed up at that first show in Houston. I figured you'd just bang her and get it over with."

Dax shook his head. "It's more than that."

"What? Are you in love or some shit like that?"

"Some shit like that," he grunted.

"Damn. Finally got tired of groupies sucking you off?"

"Screw you. She's different, Finn."

"Different how? Did she let you fuck her in the ear or something?"

"You're an asshole. I mean, I feel different when I'm around her. I like her."

"More than just for sex?"

"Yes." Dax rolled his eyes. "Is that really all it's about for you?"

"Affirmative." Finn grinned. "So, now you're gonna be pussy-whipped like Liam? What the hell kind of a band is this turning into? Are we going folk?"

"Don't worry, with your dick on the loose, our reputation will be salvaged."

"I'm only one man. Does this mean I need to nail three times as many chicks now?"

"Aren't you doing that already?" Dax pushed back his hair. "Listen, Finn. There's more to this whole thing. It's not confirmed yet, but—" His mouth snapped shut as a male voice floated into the corridor. Daxton's ears perked up. He'd heard that voice before...talking about a girl...someone who was running from something, from her past. But when—? Daxton's throat constricted when the realization hit. It was fucking Eli, and he'd been talking to Merrick about Sara when Daxton had overheard them in the green room. *Eli knew.*

"Yeah, I fucked her. She wasn't all that. Perfect ass, but not much else." *Pause.* "I'm out of here in the morning."

Pause. "Whatever. She was scared shitless and went running to that clown, Cole."

Fury coursed through Daxton's veins, making his body shake. He stormed over to the door and flung it open.

Eli's head snapped toward him, eyes wide. "Uh, hey, Dax. What's—?"

Nothing. He saw Eli's lips move and heard nothing. Seeing red was a gross understatement. All he saw was himself putting Eli through a wall. Better yet, pummeling him into the core of the earth. He grabbed Eli's shirt collar and shoved him into the cinder blocks.

"You fucking prick! You're the one who's behind all this! You're the reason Gia's in a coma!"

Finn pulled him away from Eli. "Dude, what the hell are you talking about? It was an accident."

Dax yanked out of Finn's grip, lunging for Eli again. "It wasn't an accident! This bastard did it!" He swung at Eli, the punch landing square on his jaw. "You're the one who's been sending those texts, haven't you? You tampered with the cables on stage. You almost killed Gia!"

A stream of blood drizzled from the corner of Eli's mouth. "I don't know what you're talking about. I didn't send any text, and I didn't do anything to those cables!"

"Liar!" Daxton roared, grabbing the collar of Eli's jacket. "You did this and you're the one who's gonna pay!"

"Dax!" Finn pushed him away from Eli. "Cut it out! You're acting like a fucking crazy person!"

"Get the hell out of my way, Finn! This asshole is going to fucking jail!" Daxton pushed Finn out of the way and tackled Eli to the floor. A sharp scent of antiseptic assaulted his nostrils. He pulled his arm back and swung again, his fist connecting with Eli's nose.

"I didn't do anything, Dax!" Eli tried to roll away, but Daxton caught him by the jacket again. "I don't know what you're talking about!"

"I heard you talking to Merrick about Sara! I heard you tell him about what happened in Minnesota. You're the only one who knew. The only one!"

"Dax! Leave him alone!" Finn dragged him off Eli. "Cut it out before *you're* the one who ends up in jail."

Eli clutched his nose, blood gushing down the front of his shirt. "I only told Merrick because he asked. I didn't even know anyone was texting her! She never told me, but maybe that was because she was all over your stick."

Dax took another swing at Eli, but Finn's grip was too tight. "Why the fuck should I believe that? Sara kicked you to the curb. Laney just fired your ass. You had a motive. You're the only one who would have pulled this."

Eli struggled to his feet, holding a hand over his nose. "Yeah, except I *didn't*. And it couldn't have been me fucking around with those cables because I've been staying at a hotel since Laney kicked me off the tour. Security took my access badge right after they carried me off the bus. Talk to Sean." He swayed against the wall, panting. "I'm not a fucking psychopath."

Daxton sank to his heels, leaning back against the door. If it wasn't Eli, then who the hell had access to Sara? How the fuck would someone be able to get on board her bus to leave that postcard? The texts were coming from a blocked number; it could have been the same person, but they'd need clearance to move around. The tour venues were on lockdown. Everyone needed a press pass. Even his asshat father, Sam, needed to be escorted by security to get to him. His head throbbed. "I'm sorry, man."

Eli pushed past Finn. "Fuck you, Cole. You'll be getting a call from my lawyer."

"Dude, watch it. You're bleeding all over the place. Good thing we're in a hospital." Finn snorted with laughter. "Dax, what the hell is wrong with you? He's gonna take you to the cleaners for hauling off on him like that."

"I don't care. Let him try."

"You beat the shit out of him for no reason. What the hell is up with you?"

Ten minutes and an ice pack for his swollen hand later, Daxton had gone through the sordid details, from the threatening texts and postcard to Eli screwing Laney. "How could I have known she'd thrown him off the tour? I'm not his keeper."

"Still, it doesn't make him a criminal. Just a douchebag. Did you ask Merrick about the conversation?"

"Not yet. Maybe someone else overheard them? It's not possible someone from her hometown could have gotten onto her bus to leave that postcard. Someone on the tour did it. I just don't know who. Or why."

"Are you going to beat the crap out of everyone who you think might have a reason to chase her away? Why don't you let the cops handle it?"

"I need to protect her."

Finn clapped a hand on his shoulder. "Listen, if it wasn't an accident, the cops will find the person who did it. That's what they're paid to do."

Yeah, but what if they didn't find the person in time? It had to be an inside job, but based on everything he knew, there were no leads. It's like the person disappeared into thin air without a trace. Impossible to find, until it was time to strike again.

TWENTY-SEVEN

"**D**AX, MAN. WHAT THE HELL IS UP with you? You can't just pound the shit out of people for no reason. Eli is going to sue your ass for that stunt, and the press is going to attack you like a rabid dog." Merrick handed Daxton a steaming cup of coffee. "Speaking of which, where's your little shadow? Shouldn't she be here making sure you're on your best behavior?"

"Do you have to make a dig every time you mention her name?" He glared at Merrick and poured sugar into the cup.

"You should have started with the sugar and left a little room for the coffee." Merrick snickered. "Seriously man, I don't know why you're so touchy lately. I didn't mean anything by it. Just wanted to point out that your ass is on probation with the label, and you just pummeled the other band's manager into the floor tiles."

"Ex-manager," Daxton grumbled.

"Whatever the hell you want to call him. He's still going to hang you out to dry."

"Let him try."

"Talk to me, man. Did something happen on the hiatus? You're so goddamn edgy lately. Nobody knows what to expect from you, and people are getting tired of it."

Daxton walked over to the cashier and put down the coffee. A box of grape-flavored Bubblicious gum sat on the counter. Jackpot. He looked at the young girl standing in front of the register; the one whose mouth still hadn't closed since he'd strode into the cafeteria with Merrick. "I'll take every pack you have." No response. Hell, she might not have even been breathing. *Okay, show some sign you heard me.*

She finally nodded, as if receiving his telepathic message, her eyes bugging like they were going to pop out of her food bun wrapped head. "Sure, sure, anything you want, Mr. Cole."

"Thanks. And call me Dax." He tossed his credit card on the counter and stuffed the gum into a paper bag. He nodded at the coffee in Merrick's hand. "I've got his, too."

She swiped the card once, twice, three times before taking a deep breath to steady her hand. Her cheeks flushed a deep shade of red. "Sorry," she whispered with a sheepish smile.

He grinned. "Take all the time you need."

"We just don't...I, um, I mean, there aren't a lot of

celebrities coming through here, so I guess I'm a little nervous." She bit her lower lip. "Could I get your autograph?"

"Sure thing." He scribbled his name on a scrap of paper. "What's your name?"

"Sandy." Her eyes twinkled. "Oh my gosh, this is so amazing! Thank you!"

"Anytime." He winked and picked up the coffee cup and bag of gum. Fuck the press. He could be a nice guy, and it didn't have to be for an audience. Let those assholes think what they wanted about him.

Daxton pulled out a chair at a quiet corner table and dropped into it. A long gulp of coffee made his mouth twist. "Christ, all that sugar and it still tastes like crap."

"It's hospital coffee, not Starbucks." Merrick sat across from him. "Stop avoiding the questions. You've been hunkered down with Little Miss Minnesota since we started back up. What's the deal? You fucking her or what?"

"She's going through a rough time." The next sip was worse than the first, if that was even possible. Bitter. Thick, like sludge. Fucking awful. "I'm trying to be a friend."

"Really. And what's her problem? Bunk's not big enough?"

Daxton let out a long breath. "She, uh, broke up with Eli."

"So you're nosing around for scraps? Dude…" Merrick shook his head and took a long sip of coffee.

"I'm trying to be a friend. She's upset about it and she doesn't have anyone else." Hardly plausible, but maybe Merrick would swallow it.

"Since when did you become the gay best friend?"

171

Yeah, like hell he would.

"I like her, okay? Why is that such a problem for you?"

Merrick rolled his eyes. "You *like* her? Like, as a girl-friend, like her? Does she like you, too?"

"Do you have to be such an asshole about this?"

"Yes, because you sound like a big fruitcake. Dude, why are you even wasting your time with her? She's not the girl for you."

Daxton narrowed his eyes. "What the hell is that supposed to mean?"

Merrick took a long drink from his cup, averting his eyes. "She's too pure, too wholesome. Definitely wouldn't take it up the ass. You don't do chicks like that."

The mere mention of the word conjured up images that made his cock twitch. Good God, that ass of hers was so perfect." Maybe I do now. Maybe someone like her will be good for me."

"To salvage your rep? I think the guys would appreciate that."

"It's not about the guys. Or anyone else. It's about me finding someone who actually makes me happy."

"I'm sure it'll be a refreshing change for you, Dax. Until you do something to screw it all up because we both know she's not what you need, and she'll never keep you satisfied."

Daxton slammed a hand on the table. "You're supposed to be my best friend. You've been complaining that I don't tell you anything, so here I am, trying to open up and you're—"

"Look, you're right." Merrick ran a hand through his spiky hair. "I'm sorry. If she makes you happy, then that's great. You deserve it. It's none of my business if you want to bang a choir girl. Go for it. Show some fucking stability."

He took another gulp of coffee. "Sean told me that guy showed up again."

Daxton nodded. "Yeah."

"What's his deal? Why's he on your tail?"

"He's my father."

"Fuck off."

"Nope. And the kicker? He shows up to tell me my mom is gone. She died a few weeks ago, and he thinks he can ride in on a white horse and all of a sudden be my *dad*." After another biting sip of stale coffee, he managed to relay the whole story.

"Shit, man. I'm so sorry about your mom, sorry about...everything."

"Thanks."

"Are you okay?"

"Right now, yeah. When all of this finally sinks in, who the fuck knows? I spent so much time being angry and up-set after she left. I don't know. I just feel numb."

"Did you call Tyler?"

"Not yet." Daxton rubbed his temples. "Christ, I feel like I'm about to bungee jump off a bridge. I'm standing on the edge, but I just can't take the plunge because I'm afraid the cord's gonna snap. I need time to process all this shit before I do anything."

"I get it. I'm here, Dax. If you need to talk, come find me before you beat the hell out of anyone else, okay?"

"Deal."

Merrick pushed back the chair and pulled out his

iPhone. "I've got to make some calls. You taking off?"

"Not until we get some news about Gia."

Merrick nodded toward the coffee bar. "Okay, I'm out. Listen, Coop's back there. Talk to him, man. I know you have a lot on your mind, but you need to handle this. It's been too long, and we all need to move on, okay?"

Daxton slumped back against the chair. Not the conversation he wanted to have at that moment. Or any moment, for that matter. All he wanted to do was get back to Sara, strip her naked, and bury himself inside of her to escape all of the angst surrounding him. Having a conversation with Cooper fell somewhere between getting run over by a dump truck and being mauled by a grizzly bear.

Merrick punched his shoulder. "I can see the wheels turning. Don't be such a dick. Fix this. Step one."

Cooper walked toward the table, giving Merrick a fist pump as he passed. "Mind if I sit, Dax?"

"If I say yes, will it stop you?"

"Not this time. You need to hear me out."

"Anyone ever tell you actions speak louder than words, Coop? You've made your position crystal-clear by saying absolutely *nothing*. What the hell could you possibly tell me now that will erase what you've done?"

"I was wrong on so many levels."

"'Wrong.' Interesting word choice. Fucking Jase's girlfriend while he was sick and dying, skipping his funeral, shacking up with that bitch for weeks afterward, and then radio silence? He was your best friend, you motherfucker. And you deceived him, deceived all of us! 'Wrong?'" The rage bubbled in Daxton's veins, crouched just below the surface, ready to be unleashed. "It wasn't 'wrong.' It was disgusting. *Vile.*"

"I know," Cooper whispered. Tears pooled in his eyes. "I wish I could take it all back. I didn't mean for any of it to happen. Things with Ashlee…shit, we were spending so much time together because of Jase, we just…I mean, when it happened, it was only because we were trying to comfort each other. It didn't mean anything. I never wanted it to last."

"Yet you kept fucking her for months after he died. Sure seemed like you had a thing for her skank ass."

"Things fizzled between us pretty fast. We both knew we'd made a mistake. I disappeared because I checked myself into rehab, Dax. I wasn't with Ashlee. I couldn't handle seeing Jase suffer through the chemo and surgery, and then those last few months…he was in so much pain. I was a selfish asshole, and I fell off the wagon – the needles, the pills, the booze. Christ, I was so doped up, I couldn't make it to the funeral. I barely knew what planet I was on, and I knew it would jeopardize the tour and our contract. It was my mess to clean up. Ashlee was my cover, the only one who wouldn't judge me, and would keep my secret." Cooper rubbed a hand down his stubble-peppered face. "It would have worked if the press hadn't been camped outside her place when she came to pick me up."

Daxton rubbed his temples. All that time his brother was in misery, not knowing why Cooper had pulled a disappearing act while he was at death's doorstep. Nobody knew or suspected anything until those pictures were smeared all over the tabloids afterward. "Why should your sorry ass excuses make any difference to me?"

"Because I hate myself for letting it all happen. I let my best friend down. I'll never get a chance to say good-bye because I was so fucking weak and pathetic. I gave in to my own demons while Jase was fighting his with every ounce of strength he had left. He was the brother I never had, and I couldn't handle losing him; instead, I lost myself. I'm trying so hard to get back, Dax. Please, you don't have to forgive me. I'll leave the band at the end of the tour. But I just needed you to know the truth. My actions will haunt me forever, and I'll have to live with all of my bad choices." He sniffed as he rose from the chair, tears falling from his eyes. "Not a day goes by that I don't miss him. And it's so fucking hard not to wash away all the pain and regret. But I'm trying to be strong, just like Jase was, even though it'll never be enough."

"Christ, Coop." Daxton sighed, his shoulders slumping. The pain on his friend's face was real, deep, *excruciating*. It was time to let it go. Jase was gone, and harboring so much resentment toward Cooper wouldn't change that. "Why the hell didn't you just tell me what was going on with you? You should have come to me sooner. I could have helped."

"I should have done a lot of things, Dax. I'll let the guys know this is my last leg. Thanks for listening. That's all I wanted." He turned on his heel and started for the exit.

"Stop." Daxton leaned forward, holding his head. "We've dealt with enough over the past year. We can't lose you, too."

Cooper twisted back around, his green eyes red-rimmed. "I've been lost for so long, I don't know how the hell I'm going to find my way back."

Hell, wasn't that ironic? It was exactly the way Daxton felt about his life before Sara. All the anger and resentment had eaten away at him for so long, poisoning any chance at happiness, leading him further into a maze with no exit… until he'd met Sara. She pulled him out of the quicksand that had become his suffocating existence. She was his second chance, his future, everything he had been missing for so long. Shouldn't Cooper get that same shot? Didn't he deserve a chance to make things right, to find meaning in his own life?

"Listen, we're gonna figure it out, Coop. You're not alone in this. All those times you tried to talk to me, I should have listened."

"Can we really?"

"Yeah. We can." He clapped Cooper on the back. "Come on, let's get out of here."

Jesus, was it really love that had turned him into some kind of sucker? Sure seemed like it. The void in his heart had been filled. A small smile played at Daxton's lips as he followed Cooper out of the cafeteria. He was happy. *Finally.*

TWENTY-EIGHT

"THEY'RE SAYING IT WAS AN ACCIDENT? You have to be kidding me." Daxton splashed water on his face and grabbed a hand towel from the sink ledge.

"There have been engineers and investigators here for hours, testing and searching for any indication of foul play. Nada." Sara rubbed the back of her neck. Dammit, that knot was so tight. "It's too coincidental. I was supposed to be up on stage when it happened. Someone on the inside would have known that, just like they could have gotten that postcard onto my bed."

Daxton rubbed her shoulders. "Hey. Don't worry. Security is on the alert. They're keeping it quiet, too. You're staying with me. I won't let anybody hurt you."

"But what if it's a conspiracy? Maybe the label doesn't

want law enforcement to acknowledge it wasn't an accident. That information would cause a panic and the tour would be canceled. The label would lose so much money, and—"

"Listen, the label wouldn't put two of their biggest money making bands in the line of fire. If the investigators can't find anything, it's because there's nothing to find. It doesn't mean there isn't some sicko trying to get a rise out of you. It just means said sicko isn't trying to kill you with a lighting fixture." He smirked, nudging her. "Come on, smile."

She slumped against him, letting out a deep sigh. It made sense in theory, but in reality, there was a girl with a shattered spine and assorted broken limbs lying in a hospital bed. Could it really have been a freak accident? Stranger things had happened. "I'm just glad you're back."

He tipped her head upward. "Trust me, I have lots of ideas about how we can get your mind off this crap."

"I just wish they'd found *something*. That way, the cops would have a reason to keep their eyes and ears open." She nibbled a loose cuticle.

"But they didn't, and that's a good thing. We don't need a murderer on the loose. This tour is crazy enough. After the press conference, we'll talk to the cops. I swear, nobody is going to hurt you." He brushed his lips against hers, and good Lord, for those blissful moments, she couldn't remember her own name, much less that she had an alleged stalker.

"Mmm. More please," she murmured against his ear, sliding her hands under his shirt. "Are you sure we can't hide out here in your green room just a little bit longer?"

Daxton grabbed his jacket from the couch. "Here,

maybe this will hold you over until I can get you back onto the bus." He tossed a paper bag at her.

The sweet scent of grape swirled around her nose. "Oh, yum! Thank you!"

"This is only a little taste. Something to occupy that mouth for a little while until I can take over."

She wrapped her arms around his neck. "You're incredible."

"No, I'm not." His expression sobered. "But I'm really happy, Sara. For the first time in so long, I feel good about my life and about what's ahead. It's because of you."

It was impossible. There was no way she could stop the smile from spreading across her face. "Really?" God, she was in deep with this man; the cocky rock god with a smile that could melt the panties off a nun. Could this thing between them really happen or was it just a case of tourmance? Were these feelings truly real or was this tour an alternate reality that would disappear once the media circus was over?

"Yeah." He cupped her face, his breath tickling her cheeks. "And I need you in my life because I'm in love with you."

"You're in…" She gulped, afraid to repeat the words, just in case he'd said them under some kind of spell, which might be broken if she uttered them again. "…you're in love with me?"

"Yep." He traced her cheekbone, fingers trailing a path down her neck. Her skin tingled at his soft touch. It was so good, *too* good. Oh God, if this was a dream, she never wanted to wake up. But if it wasn't, and he really did say it, where could it possibly lead?

"Are you sure, Dax? I mean, isn't this like the movies, where co-stars fall for one another because they're constantly thrown together? And then when the filming is over, so is the ride?" Her heart pounded so hard, her body shuddered from the force. "I know I'm not like any of the girls you normally date. Maybe it's just because I'm different. You *think* you feel this way but really, it's just—"

"Are you trying to convince me that I'm not in love with you?" His hands skimmed her hips, gripping them tight. She gasped as he pressed into her. God, did she want to be on her back, or in any other position, for that matter. "Exactly how much proof do you need?"

"I don't need proof, it's just…I mean, I want you to be sure because…" She inhaled, drinking in his heady scent. Cloudy with lust. That was the best way to describe her mind at that moment. Her knees buckled and she melted into his muscular embrace. *Say it, say it, say it already!* "… because I love you, too."

The corners of his lips curled upward into a wicked smirk, the gold flecks in his dark eyes glimmering with need. "So you finally admit it."

"What?" She recoiled. "You think just because you're a rock star, every breathing female is just going to automatically puddle around your mismatched socks?"

"Ouch. I didn't know my socks were such a problem for you." His grip tightened, his grin deepening. Good Lord, he was maddening sometimes. "Say it again, please."

"Which part? The one about you being a cocky rock star?" A fluttering sensation erupted in her belly, his soft lips on her neck setting her skin ablaze.

"No, the other part."

His tongue was so delicious and deviant, and just knowing they couldn't escape back to the bus until later was torture of the most delectable kind. Tiny shivers danced across the back of her neck as his mouth feasted on the sensitive area behind her ear. Never did she think that such an innocent place could make her drip with desire, but Daxton, the cocky rock god - *her* cocky rock god - knew just what buttons to press. "I love you," she breathed. "*And* your mismatched socks."

TWENTY-NINE

I T WAS HARD NOT TO LAUGH OUT LOUD. SO much for advanced degrees. Those engineers couldn't pick out a faulty cable if there was a Post-It stuck to it saying, Here I am!

The lead investigator gave his statement at the press conference in painstaking detail, explaining every check completed over the course of the day. The final assessment? Just a freak accident. Venue management must have been shitting cement blocks waiting to hear those words.

How about that? You really could find anything on YouTube. And even an amateur job was still a half-way decent one...save for one tiny detail; that fixture hadn't taken out Sara, along with that whore, Gia. One tiny change to the itinerary would have had Sara on stage, and both sluts would have been sufficiently flattened. But those damned PAs *shared a brain between them. How hard was it to print new copies for everyone? Idiots. They'd be next on the growing list.*

Sara fidgeted a few feet away in her heels. Daxton's eyes never left her, even when the press began firing questions. They were in their own little bubble, no doubt counting the seconds before they could escape back to the bus. It was so tempting to bludgeon her with a microphone stand. Stupid bitch in her slutty getups. She could never keep Daxton satisfied. He needed...no, deserved...so much more. Weren't girls from Minnesota supposed to be a bunch of prudes, anyway? What the hell was it about her that had Daxton so fucking pussy-whipped?

Or maybe the more apt question was how quickly could something be done to change that?

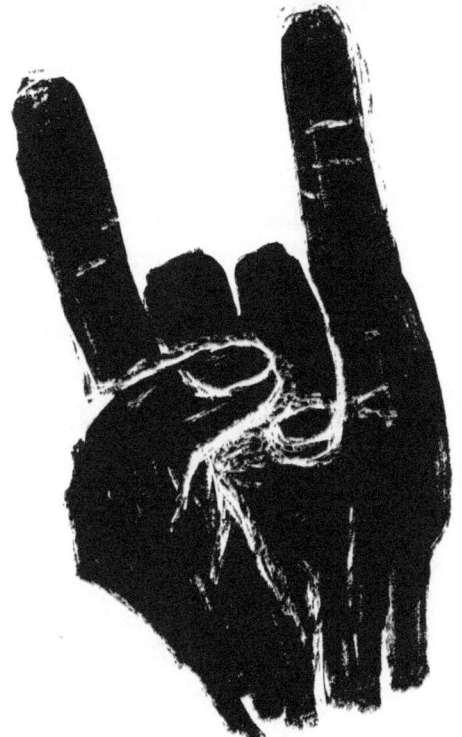

THIRTY

"H E-HELLO?" DAXTON SQUEEZED Laney's hand as she squeaked out the word. The press conference had just ended, and the security team shuttled the reporters out of the room so Laney could take a call from the hospital. Her shoulders slumped against him, mouth expelling a deep sigh. "Oh thank God! I'll be right over."

She swiped at the tears brimming in her blue eyes and smiled, probably the first real one he'd seen in a long time. "Gia's awake. She's still got a long recovery ahead of her, and lots more tests to undergo, but she's conscious."

He pulled her into his arms. "Good thing. Who else would keep you in line?"

Laney punched his shoulder. "Jerkoff."

"Bitch."

She smoothed the front of her shirt and sniffed. "Okay, I'm heading back to the hospital."

"Text me later. I'll stop by tomorrow. She'll need her rest."

Laney cocked an eyebrow. "Unlike you, right?" Her eyes flicked toward Sara, who was peering at a clipboard in Kat's hands. "So, you and the PR girl?"

"Yeah. Me and the PR girl."

"I was screwing her boyfriend."

"I heard."

"I didn't know it, though. I'm not a homewrecker."

"You've got standards, I'll give you that."

Laney tucked a strand of blonde hair behind her ear, her expression a little wistful. Ironic, considering the girl could have any guy she wanted with a snap of her perfectly manicured fingers. "You seem happy. I'm glad you've found someone, Dax. You deserve it."

"Wow, you've really turned into a sap. I'm not sure how to respond to human Laney."

"Witnessing a near-death will do that. But keep my secret. I have a reputation as a raving diva bitch to uphold, okay?"

"I'll take it to the grave."

"No pun intended. Ugh. Bad joke, I know." With a snicker, she walked toward the exit and waved at her head of security. "Okay, I'm ready to go."

Sara was still deep in conversation with Kat, probably reviewing details about the new opening band. More bad boy rockers. More headaches for the label. More questionable headlines. But at least the tour was still on. She bit her lower lip and twirled a lock of hair around her index finger. God, he wanted to scoop her up and carry her to the bus, where he'd work tirelessly to make sure every inch of her body and mind was calm and at ease. His cock twitched, as impatient as he was to get her naked.

"Hey, I heard about Gia." Cooper slapped him on the back. "That's really good news."

"Yeah. Laney took off for the hospital a minute ago."

Cooper stared at the now empty doorway before slumping against the wall. "I saw."

A smile played at Daxton's lips. "You've got a thing for her, don't you?"

"*What*? You're crazy! She's the biggest bitch I've ever met in my life. I still don't understand why the label hasn't dumped her on her ass yet." Cooper snuck a look back at the exit. Not slick enough to hide the look of longing clouding his face.

"Because she's the heart and soul of that band and has more talent in her pinkie nail than most of the pop tart ya-hoos have in their entire silicone-enhanced bodies."

With a snort, Cooper averted his eyes. "Whatever."

"Dude, it's okay to admit it. She's not banging that tool Eli anymore. Maybe you'll have a shot."

"Not interested."

"I'm fucking starving, guys! Can we please get some eats before we hit the road?" Finn barreled over with Liam and Merrick in tow.

"Eats?" Daxton snickered. "Are you looking for finger sandwiches or some shit like that?"

Finn let out a loud groan. "I haven't eaten in at least two

hours. I need sustenance."

"Ramping up for the evening's festivities?" Liam nudged him. "I'm not bunking with Coop, so you'd better have a Plan B."

Finn threw up his hands. "That's it. I'm claiming the big bedroom tonight, Dax. I'm tired of messing around on a bunk bed. There's no escape from the chicks when I want to go to sleep. They always want more. It's kind of a curse."

Sara looked up at that moment, her eyes focused on Daxton's. The corners of her pink glossed lips curled upward, as if she could see the salacious images on replay in his mind. With an exaggerated wink, it was clear she not only knew, but also was on board to re-enact them, one at a time, all night long. Kat smirked at him and exited the room, leaving Sara alone. Finally. She sauntered toward him, his groin throbbing with each swing of her slim hips. He had to channel every ounce of restraint to not pin her against the wall with the half-hard on rocking in his jeans.

"Hey, guys."

"Hey, Sara! So, what's your final assessment? Are we salvageable? Has this guy finally cleaned up his act?" Liam chuckled and took a swig of water from his bottle.

"As if that'll ever happen." Merrick cocked a pierced eyebrow.

"Give me a little credit. I'm reformed now. Now, how about you pull the pole out of your ass?" Daxton punched him in the shoulder. "And find some backup dancer to bang. That always puts you in a good mood."

A pink blush crept up the sides of Sara's face. "Well, he's still a work in progress, but much improved. Lucky for you guys, the new opening band has a lot more notoriety. Their PR team doesn't sleep at *all*."

Daxton snickered and slung an arm around her waist. "Yeah, and about that last request, Finn? You'd damned better have a Plan B because the back bedroom is off-limits."

Finn laughed. "I guess that means you're eating someone…er, I mean, *with* someone else tonight."

"You guessed right." He tightened his grip around Sara. "Maybe I'll catch you guys for breakfast."

"Not if I have anything to say about it," Sara murmured against his ear.

The throbbing intensified. Fuck food. He only needed one form of nourishment, stripped down and on her back. Immediately, if not sooner.

"Come on, guys." Finn smirked. "I don't want to be responsible for cock-blocking our bro."

Daxton grasped Sara's hand. "Much obliged, Finn." He nodded at Merrick, who'd stalked over to a corner, speaking into his phone in a hushed tone. "What's his deal? Did someone forget to give him his happy pill?"

Liam rolled his eyes and drained the last of his water. "He's a bigger diva than you, man. Probably on the rag. Don't worry, I'm babysitting tonight. You kids have fun. Try not to scream too loud. If I'm not hammered enough to pass out, I don't want to have to listen to you fornicating all night long."

Sara clapped a hand over her mouth. God, she was so fucking adorable. He couldn't wait to make the walls of that bus shake. The two-minute walk to the parking lot was even too long.

"I'd get some earplugs if I were you." Daxton winked at him and pulled Sara toward the exit. "Come on, gorgeous. Don't look so horrified. I'd never make them believe we were playing video games with the way you sing."

"Oh my gosh! You are so horrible!"

His steps quickened. The arena exit was finally in sight. Security lined the perimeter. Nobody was getting through that human wall. "Really? That's not what you were screaming last night. If memory serves, you were calling me God Almighty. A *lot*."

THIRTY-ONE

OH GOD, THOSE LIPS. IT WAS ALMOST as if they were sizzling coils heating every square inch of her overly sensitized body. She gripped the bed sheets tightly, each shallow breath catching in her throat. "Dax," she whispered. "*Please*. Don't make me wait."

"But waiting is so much fun," he murmured, the vibrations of his husky voice tickling her navel. His teeth closed around her pink lace thong and, with a yank, the delicate fabric tore from her body.

"You're gonna pay for those," she panted.

"I have an idea. Stop wearing them." He let out a low moan. "Oh fuck, knowing what I'd have clear access to, all the time…"

"Mmm. Sounds tempting." Her fingers traced over the ink covering his muscled biceps. She sank into the plush mattress with a loud gasp, her heart thrumming as his devious tongue dipped into her wetness, lapping up every drop of latent desire. It brushed over her swollen clit, once, twice, three times before delving into her heat. It was a torturous move, just enough to make her drip with longing and plead for release. Every nip and lick catapulted her closer to the brink. Powerful hands gripped her backside, squeezing the flesh, forcing her body upward for leverage. Tears sprung to her eyes as the orgasm tore through her. Singing was probably an understatement, since she was only a few high notes shy of shattering glass at that point.

Aftershocks rippled through her like all-consuming waves, calmed only by his lips; the ones searing a path back to her mouth. They pressed against hers, soft and gentle, yet so very greedy...*insatiable*. His ruthless tongue tantalized, tangling with her own, flooding her insides with lust. This man, who'd thought he was so broken, had been the only one able to piece her shattered heart back together, and he'd given her everything that eluded her for so long - faith, hope, and *love*.

His cock swelled between her legs, her body screaming to be filled with everything he had to give. She wouldn't be...*couldn't* be...complete without him, without feeling their connection, without immersing herself into all that was Daxton Cole.

"I love you," he breathed. His arms snaked around her torso, gripping her tightly. The head of his cock toyed with her slit, rubbing, taunting, teasing...his signature devious play. Sharp, shallow breaths were all she could muster as she gripped his hips in sheer agony, pressing them against her fevered skin. She shuddered, anticipation flooding her extremities until he finally slid inside, stretching her, filling her with every inch of his desire. Their flushed, frenzied bodies, slick with sweat, rocked together, moment after blissful moment. As much as her body craved release, the intoxicating sensations crashing over her were too addictive. *Never let it stop.*

Each thrust was deeper than the last, his perfect cock burrowing farther into her depths, pulsating faster and harder until she writhed under him. Tremors rumbled within, gathering speed and intensity like a boulder careening down a mountain. Her mind was a blank canvas, all coherent thoughts immersed in the explosion that commanded her, firing every last nerve ending. His hungry mouth silenced her screams, muting the piercing sounds. With one final thrust, he shuddered against her, gripping her tight.

She buried her head in his neck, still panting, still consumed by his heady scent. Minutes turned into hours, their bodies entwined. It wasn't long enough. *Forever* would never be enough.

Daxton squinted in the darkness. Only a small sliver of moonlight crept into the room through the closed curtains. It must be the middle of the night. Time didn't matter, though. Sara shifted farther into him with a deep sigh. Her bare skin was so soft and smooth against his. She looped her ankle around his, pulling herself even deeper into his embrace. His hands refused to behave, his body way to sensitized to drift off again. Her firm backside slid against his cock, now rock-hard, fully awake, and in desperate need of some recognition.

It was impossible to keep his hands away from her supple skin. He brushed the back of her neck with his lips. God, he was hungry, and Sara was the only sustenance his body would consume. When his hand traced a very determined path down to her navel, she let out a soft moan and guided it right between her thighs. His cock twitched as his fingers plunged into her slick opening, pausing only to rub her swollen clit.

"Dax, don't tease me anymore," she breathed, her body shuddering against him. "I need you. *Now*."

As if he needed any more prompting.

He grabbed a condom from the nightstand and rolled it on before sinking into her heat. Her walls clenched, sucking him deeper. It was impossible to form a coherent thought. Her movements muted every functional brain cell. He nipped her shoulder, trailing his tongue across her neck to the sensitive area behind her ear. Their bodies slapped together, her juices flowing over his fingers with each stroke of her nub. She thrust backward, faster, and harder, her body begging him for release.

His cock throbbed, unable to be sated. Adrenaline coursed through him. He needed more, everything that she had to give. He slid out, separating the globes of her perfect ass then rubbing himself around the rim of her hot channel. He groped around in the dark for the jar of coconut oil on the nightstand. With a flick of his wrist, the top spun off, and he dug his fingers into the thick consistency. The warmth of his skin liquefied the oil. With slow strokes, he massaged her tight hole, rubbing the oil around the rim before inserting one finger.

She gasped, her back arching, beckoning him.

"Does that hurt?" he murmured, his lips nuzzling her neck.

"No, just don't stop touching me."

He opened her with a second finger, stretching her, making her whole body clench until she was ready for him. Another scoop of the scented oil, a few strokes of his dick, and it was time. He rubbed the swollen head along the opening before removing his fingers and sliding inside her. Christ, it was erotic as all hell, knowing she fully trusted him with something so intimate, yet *so* taboo. She moved against his cock, allowing him deeper access. Her body grew frenzied with every pulse, gripping him tighter as the minutes passed. Tremors shot through him, and his eyes squeezed shut, as blood rushed to his groin. He was on the brink, grasping her hips, barely able to squeeze out a breath. It didn't matter. He could die right then; the sensations were that incredible.

Her cries pierced the silence. Each thrust of her body against his brought him closer to the edge, and he wanted nothing more than to leap. His breath stilted until the explosion from deep within his core erupted, firing every nerve ending. The release was like nothing he'd ever experienced. He filled her with all he had, all she'd dragged out of him. The passing seconds were mind numbing. Being with Sara, falling in love with her, and connecting with her on every possible level was all he'd ever needed, and everything he'd ever wanted. Forever.

THIRTY-TWO

"Mmm. Don't move, okay? Just ignore it."

Sara's ringtone blared again. "It's Kat. You know she won't stop calling until I answer."

Daxton pulled her closer. "I don't care."

"You say that now." She snuggled against him, her velvety soft skin blanketing him in warmth that he could never get from blankets alone.

Goddamn chimes sounded for the fiftieth time. Who would've thought that an innocuous enough ringtone could make someone want to hurl a phone against a brick wall?

"Ahh! Fine! Get it already!"

Sara giggled. "Told you." She grabbed the phone from the nightstand. "Hey, Kat. What's up?"

The call meant one thing – playtime was over for the

foreseeable future. It was back to the real world, where fun with coconut oil was put on hold; at least, until after tonight's show. He let out a deep sigh, trailing his fingers down the smooth column of her spine, reveling in the way she shivered against him. Well, his cock definitely enjoyed it, rubbing along the crack of her perfect ass. It was so tempting to fling that phone across the room and plunge himself deep into her heat.

"Okay. Yes, give me about twenty minutes. I'll take care of it." Sara clicked off the phone and flipped over. Her lips were deep pink, courtesy of his early morning nibbling.

"What happens in twenty minutes?"

"Kat needs some promo pics to blast out on social media. I need to get everything staged, which means you need to get your butt up, too."

"Speaking of butts…"

Her cheeks flushed a deep shade of purple. He smirked. Kind of reminded him of her prized grape-flavored gum. Was it possible to be insanely sexy and adorable at the same time? Guess so.

"How are you feeling? Are you sore?"

"A little, but it's fine." Her eyes dropped. "I really liked it."

Oh, fuck yeah. Her tight, hot channel, squeezing his cock as he slid in and out, playing with her clit, making her scream with each thrust…it was nothing short of amazing.

"I've got plenty of coconut oil."

She giggled. "I'm not surprised. Maybe we can do something with it later?"

"If you keep talking like this, there won't be a later.

There will only be a right now."

His fingers tangled in her blonde waves, lips pressed against hers. "Open your legs for me. I need you right now," he murmured against her ear.

Her legs fell open, inviting him to sink into her depths. He stroked himself a couple of times and rolled on a condom. She let out a gasp as he slid inside her slick, velvety walls. His cock throbbed with each thrust into her tight pussy, his balls tightening with each passing second. He grasped the globes of her ass, squeezing the plump cheeks, forcing himself deeper. Unable to breathe, drowning in lust...love...some combination of both. Whatever it was, he never wanted to be resuscitated. Her muscles clamped around him, forcing him deeper.

Thump, thump, thump!

Her soft whimpers turned into cries begging him to make her come.

Thump, thump, thump!

What the fuck was that pounding?

"Dax!"

Sara clapped a hand over her mouth.

"Finn, what the hell? I'm busy!"

"Yeah, I know. So does everyone else on the bus. Including your dad."

His dad? Fucking *Tyler*?

"Um, you might want to come out here."

If Sara's eyes bugged out any more, he was pretty sure her eyeballs would just pop out of her head. "It's okay," he whispered.

"But your dad is *here*! And I was just screaming for you

to make me come! And I'm *naked*!"

He grinned and brushed his lips against her forehead. "This is all true. Just relax, okay. I'll take care of everything. Just don't get dressed. I want that pussy to be screaming for me again, got it?"

"I'm pretty sure that won't be an issue."

A pair of basketball shorts had been flung over a corner chair. He grabbed them and yanked a tank top over his head. Where the hell was his baseball cap?

"It's on the night table," Sara whispered, pointing to where it sat, right next to the jar of coconut oil.

He flipped the cap around before putting it on his head. "Be ready."

Just seeing that jar of coconut oil made his cock twitch. Fucking blue balls. Damn Tyler. Why the hell was he here, anyway? He clenched his fists as he walked into the common area. Did Sam go to the press?

"What are you doing here, *Dad*?"

Tyler stood against the bar, his face clouded over with a mix of emotions Daxton had never before witnessed - pain, remorse, regret. Why now, when everything was upside down? Why hadn't he displayed any degree of feeling before, when he had every opportunity to make things right between them? "Sam called. He told me he spoke to you. I guess he didn't want to take a chance that the press might find out first and run with a story before I found out."

"That was big of him. So now, after all this time, you decide to drop by for a visit. To do what? Make sure I'm okay? Like you ever gave a shit before?" The fury he'd been bottling up for the past twenty-four hours burst from deep within his soul. "Were you ever going to tell me the truth? Mom left, and you never told me why. She *died* and you never said a word!" He hurled an open bottle of water across the room, liquid splashing out of the top, soaking the carpet. "Why? Make me understand *why*, goddammit!"

Tyler sank into the couch, holding his head in his hands. "Daxton, I—"

"You what? You were afraid of getting your ego pricked because your wife was screwing another guy, so you paid him to disappear and adopted the bastard son? Did you ever want me? Why did you make him give me up? Maybe he would have loved me, treated me like a real son. But you made sure that didn't happen!"

"Dax, I never wanted you to find out like this. Yes, it was hard for me to deal with your mother's infidelity. But dammit, I loved her and wanted to make things between us work. Sam didn't have a pot to piss in when she got pregnant. I adopted you because I wanted to give you everything he couldn't. I did the best I could to hold things together, but after Jase died, your mom wanted to leave. I found out later that she got sick. She didn't even tell me until her days were numbered."

"Sam wanted me to forgive him, so we could start fresh." Daxton gritted his teeth.

"What did you tell him?" Tyler looked up, his face drawn and haggard, almost as if he'd aged ten years in the past five minutes.

"I told him he missed his chance when he walked away. I have no desire to start a relationship with the man who gave me up. I don't care what his reasons were." Daxton scrubbed a hand down his stubble-peppered face. "But you? You've always had it out for me. Is it because I was a constant reminder that she'd cheated? Is that why you never gave a shit?"

Tyler rose from the couch. "Dax, stop it. I know I haven't always been the best father, but you're not free from blame in this. You were the one who pulled away. You were so goddamn stubborn through the years, rejecting every attempt I made to have any sort of relationship with you. I've given you everything. And when Jase got sick, yeah, it was devastating, and yes, he was my focus; not because he was my biological son, but because he needed me. You have no idea how it feels to lose a child. I hope you never find out. I was emotionally gutted when he died. Things were already hard, then your mom left and you just kept twisting the knife. I was angry, guilt-ridden, and heartbroken." He raked a hand through his hair. "I should have tried harder. I regret my past actions every day. It was my responsibility to take care of you, and I let you down. We let each other down. That's why I'm here, Dax. When Sam called, it killed me to think you'd choose to have him in your life over me. I knew I needed to make things right between us. At least, I had to try."

Daxton pressed his hands to his throbbing temples. He'd been difficult. Hell, he'd been a complete asshole. But it was his way of coping with the nagging feeling that he didn't fit, that he wasn't good enough for Tyler. "I could never make you happy, no matter what I did. Do you have any idea how miserable I was, how worthless I felt?'

"I'm sorry."

"That's all? That's supposed to erase all the bad shit, Dad?" Daxton pounded his fist against the wall.

"I can't change the past, Dax. I can't take back all the pain I caused you. But I want to fix this, to fix *us*."

"Why didn't you tell me all this before?"

"Because I was hurt and angry, too. You've taken every opportunity to tear me down - face to face, in the press. I know I made a lot of mistakes over the years, but I want to move forward. You're my son, and I love you. We've never seen eye to eye, and maybe we never will, but we're all we have left. Isn't that worth anything to you?"

Rejection and spite had corrupted him for so long, too long. Love made him realize what he'd been missing, but it couldn't fully heal the still raw wounds. No, only the truth could mend him and make him whole again.

"Yeah." His throat tightened, tears gathering at the corners of his eyes. God, it hurt so bad. Losing his mom and Jase...the grief was crippling. He needed Tyler, his father. They needed each other. Enough time had been wasted.

Tyler pulled him into a tight hug. "I'm so sorry for letting things get this far. Give me a chance to be the father you deserve, Dax."

"I'm sorry, too." Daxton pulled away, expelling a deep breath. "We were both pretty shitty to one another."

Tyler nodded slowly, a pained expression etched into his features. "Please, Dax. I've already lost so much. I can't lose you, too."

Hope flickered in Daxton's heart. He'd lived without it for so long, and now that it was alive once again, he never wanted to lose it. "We have a lot to catch up on, Dad."

"Yes, we do." Tyler smiled. "I'm glad we finally agree on something."

"Maybe we can have dinner after the show. There's someone I want you to meet. Someone really important." He glanced at the closed bedroom door and then back at Tyler, a grin lifting his lips. "Later."

Tyler cocked an eyebrow. "Judging by the sounds coming from there a little while ago, I'll take that to mean *much* later."

THIRTY-THREE

HOT WATER EXPLODED FROM THE showerhead, doing nothing to relieve the ache deep within his groin. *Fuck, he wanted to feel those lips clamped around his throbbing cock, sucking him dry. And that ass...plunging into the hot, tight channel, burying himself inside that forbidden area, filling it with his hot seed...*

He pumped his hand faster, shivering against the chill. *His body shuddered against the tile, balls tightening, imagining only those lips pressed against his. He'd been waiting so long...too long to taste. All those days and nights spent watching, wondering, and longing for his chance. Waiting was no longer an option. He craved too much.*

White light exploded behind his eyes as the orgasm consumed him. His heart thrummed, the sensations coursing through him blunted the reality that the one he so desired was in love with another.

He climbed out of the shower and grabbed a thick towel. After tonight, no obstacles would remain. He'd have exactly what he wanted, on his terms. Nobody would ever stand in his way ever again. Didn't he deserve to be happy with the one person he loved more than anything?

Soon, the whole world would know they were destined to be together. And as best friends, was there a better way to start a relationship?

Merrick smiled at his reflection in the fogged up mirror. The one remaining loose end would be tied up soon enough. Then, Dax would be his. Forever.

THIRTY-FOUR

"STOP BITING YOUR NAILS. THERE ISN'T any more nail polish on them, and pretty soon you'll be chewing your fingers." Daxton pulled a grape-flavored Capri Sun juice pouch out of the refrigerator in his green room and handed it to Sara. "Will this make you feel any better?"

If the room had been dim before, it was now illuminated with Sara's megawatt smile. "A tiny bit. Thank you."

"Why are you so nervous? It's just my dad."

Her cheeks flooded with color, matching the shade of juice she sucked from the straw. "Um, yeah, just your dad, who happened to overhear me screaming my friggin' head off while we were making love. No reason for me to feel anything other than confident and self-assured. Slutty? Never."

Daxton placed his hands on her shoulders. "Would it make you feel better if I told you he's caught me in much more compromising positions?"

Her eyes widened, as she sputtered out a very emphatic, "No! Oh my God, I can't believe…no, wait. I totally can."

He snickered. "What does that say about you?"

"Oh, it speaks volumes about me." The deep flush lightened, her tone turning serious. "But how are *you* doing?"

"Hey, don't worry about me. You're my priority now." He trailed a fingertip over her cheekbone and over her purple-tinged lips. Earlier that day, he'd told Sara everything about Sam, his mom, and the blowout with Tyler. He'd never opened up to anyone like he had to Sara. Hell, he'd never had someone to confide in, someone who actually cared enough to listen. She had the power to heal him, to comfort him, and to piece him back together. "Nothing else matters right now."

"Dax, don't you think you need time to grieve? You can't keep everything bottled up. It'll destroy you. Let me help you through this." Her eyes searched his, begging to see what hid deep within the recesses of his soul.

What Sara didn't realize was that she'd already saved him from drowning in his own sorrow. Nobody could ever take the place of family he'd lost, but his love for Sara was all-consuming, and hope for their future propelled him through the grief.

"I miss my mother, Sara. She left, and it devastated me. Every day, I got angrier and angrier that she could abandon our family. I understand now that she was trying to protect me from having to watch her suffer like Jase did. And even though I resent her for making the decision to walk away, I can move forward because I know she's not ever coming back. I'll never get closure, and I have to accept that. She'll never know how much worse it was to lose her while she was still alive, when I could have been with her every step of the way, loving her and taking care of her until the very end. It still hurts really fucking badly, and that pain isn't going away any time soon." He smoothed back her hair, the glossy waves so soft against his skin. "But it also makes me want to take advantage of what I have right now. I'm not willing to waste even a second with you because each one is precious. I'm crazy about you, Sara. You've already helped me more than you know."

Her green eyes glittered with unshed tears, a bright spot of pink settling into the tip of her nose.

"You know you look like Rudolph when you're about to cry, right?"

A soft chuckle escaped her lips as the tears streamed down her face. "Thank you for being so observant. You really know how to charm a girl. How, oh how, did I get so lucky?"

"If you feel that way now, just wait until later."

Thump, thump, thump.

Sara recoiled with a gasp, all of the color from her flushed cheeks draining in a blink. "Cheese and crackers," she whispered.

"Is it safe to come in?" Tyler's deep baritone held a hint of amusement. At least it did to Daxton.

"Yeah, Dad," he called out, running a hand over her backside, giving it a hard squeeze before opening the door.

"Mmm. Just *wait*."

He opened the door to find his father with an all-knowing smirk spread across his face. Tyler pulled him in for a tight hug. It felt nice, secure, comforting. "Glad I wasn't interrupting this time."

Daxton's eyes flicked over toward Sara, who looked as if she might have a stroke at any second. "Dad, this is Sara. She's our new publicist. And my girlfriend."

"So you're the young lady I've been waiting to meet. It's a pleasure." Tyler grasped her hand, raising it to his lips. Even at fifty, he was smooth enough to charm women out of their panties. At least now, Sara was blushing for a different reason.

"Mr. Cole, it's um, really an honor to meet you." She flashed a shy smile. Her hand twitched and Daxton knew she was aching to nibble at her fingernails. She was so sweet and innocent, but so very bad at the same time. He shifted to reposition his half hard-on. The fact that his father was standing only a couple of inches away should have made his dick limp as a noodle, but her presence was like a shot of adrenaline to the heart…if his heart was in his pants.

"Please call me Tyler. Mr. Cole just makes me sound old." He smirked. "I'm sure these guys are really making you earn your paycheck."

"When my boss said prepare to work around the clock, I didn't realize he was serious." A giggle tumbled from her lips, then her eyes popped open wide as realization set in. "Oh, um, I didn't mean it like that. I just, uh… I meant…"

"She had no idea how high-maintenance we all were." Daxton winked at her.

"Just a word of advice. Next time ask for more money. These rock stars can be real troublemakers." Tyler grinned. "Especially this guy."

"Thanks for the tip." Her phone pinged. "Oh, shoot. Dax, we need to move. Punk'd just finished their opening set. Mr. Cole...er, Tyler, would you like to watch the concert from the VIP viewing area?"

"As long as you'll be accompanying me. Can't say I'm not curious to find out more about the woman who's turned my son inside out." He pointed to Daxton. "See that look? I know I haven't before now."

"Just watch the show, okay, Dad? Keep the talking to a minimum. I'd like her to stick around for a while."

Tyler chuckled. "I'm not promising anything. Anyway, all of your skeletons are public. If she hasn't run yet, you're probably safe."

"Thanks for the vote of confidence."

Tyler pulled out his buzzing iPhone. "Excuse me for a second, kids. I need to take this."

Daxton pulled Sara into his arms and backed her against the couch. "How long do you think we have before he comes back?"

"Not nearly enough time. But don't worry, I'm not going anywhere. At least, not until after the show," she murmured against his ear, her hand sliding over the bulge in his jeans.

"Dirty girl."

"*Your* dirty girl."

He let out a groan. "And torturing me is fun for you?"

"Oh it's entertaining as hell, but not nearly as much as

some other things I can be doing to you. *Will* be doing to you."

His cock swelled as her grip tightened. Damn jeans were so constricting; they had no give at all. "Don't tease me. *Show* me."

"Later. You need to handle *that*," she said, waving her hand around his aching groin. "And then get your sexy butt on stage."

"Dax! I know you're in there! Are you coming or what?" Finn's booming voice came from outside the door. Like a tornado, he blew in, a wicked smirk on his face. "Oh shit. I guess you are. At least, you look pretty close."

Daxton shoved Finn out the door. "Enough. Let's go." He wrapped an arm around Sara and headed into the crowded corridor where Sean and the rest of the bodyguards waited. Security was tight since there was still a psycho on the loose. The label wasn't taking any more chances with its talent; plus, Tyler traveled with his own armed entourage. Sara would be safe, and she was his biggest concern.

Equipment teams for Punk'd rushed to break down the stage setups once they were wheeled into the hallway. Another team of security surrounded the band members, escorting them along with a gaggle of half-naked girls back toward the suite of rooms.

"Papa Ty! I heard you were here. Looking forward to the wedding." Finn clapped a hand on Tyler's back. "And to the bridesmaids."

"I'm sure you are. Just make sure none of them end up on YouTube or I'll make sure you're violated with those drumsticks. Got it?"

"I love this guy!" Finn rubbed Tyler's shoulders as they walked into the backstage area. "Don't look so tense, Ty. I'll make sure the wedding is over before I pull out the video camera."

"Oh no, I forgot my phone!" Sara slapped her hands against her legs. "I'll be right back, okay?"

"Forget it, beautiful. You're not going back there by yourself. I'll get it." Daxton grasped her wrist.

Finn snorted. "Don't even think about it, lover boy. You need to get your ass on stage. Tell Merrick to get it if you're so afraid."

"It'll just take a minute. I'll be fine." Daxton looked at Sean. "Stay with Sara and Tyler. Don't let anyone near them."

Sean nodded. "You got it, Dax." His beefy frame shifted, fencing them in. Nobody was breaking through that human barrier. Shit, they were barely even visible over his hulking shoulders.

Daxton jogged down the empty corridor and around the corner toward his green room. Punk'd was in a separate section of the maze, and they took most of the noisy party along with them. All the crews for Jimmy Sixx were on point to handle stage and sound setup.

He pulled out his key and turned it in the lock. The door opened, the room blanketed in darkness. Where the hell was the light switch? He lost his balance, stumbling into what felt like a table as the door slammed shut.

A strong hand clamped over his mouth. Any discernible sounds he could make were held prisoner. His throat tightened, body aching to draw in a breath. A powerful force impaled his chest, like a hot poker searing a path through his insides. A crippling tingle ravaged his midsection, almost as if his body was being electrocuted, consumed by a heat so intense, it might just spontaneously combust at any second. The assailant tugged at the weapon, the serrated edges tearing apart his flesh like razor blades raking over bare skin.

Daxton's knees buckled and he collapsed onto the carpet. A warm, sticky liquid soaked his t-shirt, pooling around him. He tasted metal…his blood. "Who the hell are you?" he choked. His mouth was bone-dry, teeth chattering like he was trapped in a freezer. Violent tremors assaulted his body, an icy coldness slithering through him. Death. This was the end. And the attacker? For all he knew, it was the grim fucking reaper, who had shredded his chest with a sickle. He needed to get up, to scream, to run. Where was everyone? Couldn't anybody save him?

His eyes clouded over, bile rising in his throat. Waves of nausea pummeled him, his stomach ready to revolt at any second. There was no hope of moving; his limbs were all frozen, imaginary cement blocks weighing down his body. He was numb, immobile, and completely fucked.

One last foggy thought flashed through his mind before his eyelids drooped closed. *Who's going to save Sara?*

THIRTY-FIVE

I T WAS HARD TO DESCRIBE THE CHARGE OF
elation that had flowed through him when the knife
impaled Sara's chest. He knew she'd eventually be
back looking for her phone, the one he'd palmed earlier.
Stupid bitch had it coming, just like those other skanks and
their little "accidents." But then he heard Daxton's voice,
drenched in anguish and desperation. What the fuck? He
was supposed to be on stage already!

A flick of the light switch made Merrick crumble to the
floor next to the bloody puddle surrounding the man he
needed as much as air, food, and water. "Dax! Fuck!"

He dropped the knife and grasped Daxton's hand. It
was stiff, cold, almost as if—No! Not now. Not when they
were so close.

"God, please! I can't lose you, Dax. I love you." He

pressed his ear against Daxton's chest. Nothing, except a seemingly endless flow of blood gushing from the wound. *No, no, no!*

A rapid escape was unfathomable. Leaving Daxton... not knowing if he'd just killed the love of his life...

He grabbed the knife and plunged it into his thigh. "Ahh!" Searing pain exploded down his leg, but it was nothing compared to the agony of seeing Daxton clinging to life at his own hand. It wasn't enough. He needed to feel more, to let the anguish consume him for what he'd done. Gripping the handle, he jammed the blade into his side. Christ, there was so much blood.

He wiped the handle of the knife with his jacket lining and slithered toward the couch. Numbness snaked through his insides, paralyzing his ability to move, to think, to weep. Tears blurred his vision. "Help," he croaked. "Please help."

THIRTY-SIX

"SARA, THESE PRE-SHOW SHOTS ARE fantastic. They're blowing up on Instagram. I'm already showing thirty thousand likes, and they were only posted an hour ago." Kat shoved her iPhone screen in Sara's face. "Unprecedented!"

"That's awesome." She rubbed the back of her neck. Something was off, but it was evading her. Where was Tyler? Her eyes scouted the darkened space. Hordes of record executives, publicists, agents, and A-listers swarmed the suite, and it was hard to think above the commotion. Nope, he was there, surrounded by doting female fans, none above the age of twenty.

"What's wrong with your neck? Did Dax have you in some crazy ass position?" Kat snickered. "Wait, don't answer. I really don't want to know."

A strange feeling settled in her belly. Uneasiness? Nerves? It definitely wasn't due to the cluster of butterflies that took flight whenever Daxton's name was mentioned. "I just…I don't know. Maybe it's a stress knot."

"Mm-hm." Kat cocked an eyebrow. "Maybe he can rub out your stress knot *later.*"

Sara peered through the large glass pane overlooking the stage and then at her watch. Ten minutes had passed. How long would it have taken him to grab the phone and get backstage? A thudding in her chest grew more intense with each passing second. "Excuse me for a second, Kat." She walked over to Sean, gnawing at her thumbnail. "Hey, Dax has been gone for a while. I'm going to check on him."

"No, he wanted you to stay put. I'll send one of the guys to the green room." Sean pulled out his walkie-talkie.

"Please, let me just go. I'll be careful. Maybe he's in the bathroom." She forced out a half-hearted giggle, desperate to ignore the chill that seeped through her insides. This was all wrong. He would have brought the phone to her or at least sent someone else. Too much time had passed. If something had happened to him…

"Please, stay here, Sara. Let me—"

"No." She pushed past him and shoved open the door. "You can send them after me, but I'm going." A sob rose in her chest, her heels clicking on the concrete floors of the arena corridors with each sprint. The door to his green room was closed. She gripped the handle and pushed it open, blood rushing between her ears. *Oh God, please let him be okay. Please, please, please.*

The green room door slammed open. A strangled cry resounded in the expanse, followed by shrieks for help. Bright fluorescent lights from the hallway illuminated the space. His eyes opened a crack to see Sara crumble to the floor next to Dax. Merrick shifted his aching body, pain slicing through his now-jagged insides. He'd fallen unconscious behind the sofa, out of her view, so she couldn't have seen him unless she ventured farther inside.

"Dax! Oh God! Dax!" Sara's voice pierced his brain. Merrick clutched his temples, the high-pitched sound reverberating through him. "Please wake up!"

Nothing. No response. A chill slithered through him despite the numbness setting into his limbs. *Say something Dax. Please.*

Fucking bitch. She was supposed to be lying there. Dead! Out of his life. Out of his way!

Sean ran into the room, dropping to the floor next to Sara.

"Is he going to be okay? He isn't moving, Sean. Please help him!"

Merrick pressed his hand against the self-inflicted gash in his side. Blood poured from the wound. Fuck, he must have nicked something important. "Help me," he croaked.

Five medics rushed into the room with bags of equipment minutes after Sean's call for help, descending on Dax. He was the star of the show, after all. Who the fuck cared about the lovesick manager who might just be bleeding to death himself?

He watched Sara grasp Dax's hand, shoulders quaking. Her lips were moving pretty fast. Maybe she was praying. *She should be.*

"We've got a pulse! He's alive." The welcome words permeated the thick fog surrounding Merrick's mind. The medics cheered. "Let's get him out to the ambulance."

"Oh thank God!" Sara's raspy voice rose, relief lacing her words. "Sean, can you get Tyler? He's still back in the suite."

Dax was alive. Thank fucking God. Merrick tried to slither closer, but his head was as heavy as a block of cement, impossible to raise, even the slightest bit. Shit, he'd lost so much blood. All sounds faded, morphing into white noise. His body felt like it was floating above the carpet, levitating, away from the agony he'd just inflicted upon himself and the man he adored.

A medic hovered over Merrick, shouting questions about the attacker and the weapon lying next to him, but his mouth refused to form words in response. His brain couldn't string together a single coherent thought. His fingers and toes tingled with the sensation of being pricked with pins and needles. The medic snapped his fingers, his face blurred, and then warmth. A welcome heat, one that flowed throughout his extremities, replaced the frigid chill that had previously accosted his body.

Dax was safe. He could finally rest.

THIRTY-SEVEN

Two months later...

THE MASSIVE SWELLS OF THE PACIFIC Ocean crashed against the cliff overlooking the horizon. The setting sun provided an orange glow, soft rays reflecting off the glittering waters below. High walls of exotic flowers and foliage created a natural barrier to any paparazzi who dared creep close enough to snap a picture. And if the barricades didn't deter them, the armed guards lining every corner were sure to send them running with their cameras swinging between their legs.

A deep breath filled Sara's lungs. The scent of the sea air provided serenity and peace, something they'd been lacking for the past couple of months since the attack. Those chilling moments, finding Daxton unconscious, drenched in blood, not knowing if she'd lost the love of her life...

the haunting sequence of events was never too far into her subconscious to rear its ugly head. Nightmares plagued her since that night, the fear of losing the one person she needed more than food or air was constant.

But tonight, all fears were put on the back burner. It was a celebration, of the most epic variety.

"Have I told you how gorgeous you look?" Daxton's warm breath fluttered against her cheek, tickling her skin like soft feathers.

"Yes, but I never get tired of hearing it, so if you feel the need to repeat yourself, please do."

"You look gorgeous tonight." The corners of his lips curled upward. "Although, I can't wait to strip you out of that dress later."

She bit her lip. "Are you sure?"

"Yes." He snaked an arm around her waist. "The doctor said it's perfectly fine. You were there."

"I know, but I'm afraid. What if you rupture something? That could still happen months after the injury. You could die of internal bleeding before we even know there's a problem! Maybe we should wait a little longer, just go to one more doctor."

"No way. I can't hang on another second. In fact, I'm thinking about running you up to the house now. There are plenty of bedrooms to choose from." He winked. "What do you say?"

"I'm scared. If something happened to you…I just…I can't lose you, Dax."

"Hey." He cupped her chin, tilting it upward. His heady scent swirled around her head like a halo, making her woozy with repressed lust. "I'm not going anywhere. I promise. And if you don't feel comfortable, we'll wait." He let out a deep sigh. "Although seeing you dance around in those lace thongs and matching bras every day is making me die a slow, torturous death. Worse than the threat of any rupture."

She giggled. "I didn't realize you watched so closely."

"I'm a pretty observant guy." His soft lips brushed against her forehead. "You win. We'll go to the doctor on Monday. And once he says there are no risks, I'm tearing off those panties with my teeth, got it?"

"Got it. I know how much you love that." A chill zipped through her, his half-hooded gaze damn-near melting off the lace panties in question. The guy could sizzle her insides with nothing more than a suggestive wink. Jeez, was she ever weak. She slid an arm around his waist, silently cursing her choice of shoes. One false move, and her heels would be held prisoner by the cobblestones along their path back to the reception.

A soft breeze swept through the thin material of her gown. She shivered against Daxton's shoulder. A deep breath filled her with desire. That cologne; it was her favorite. The mere thought of burying her head into his neck, inhaling his essence…good Lord, and she was supposed to be the chaste one?

"How about some champagne?" he murmured against her ear.

Champagne and a cold shower, thank you very much. The bar was only a few feet away. It wasn't like she could jump his bones right out in the open. Too many iPhones…

and Tyler probably wouldn't appreciate having the focus off Layla, his blushing young bride. "Sure."

Finn's booming voice rang out over her shoulder, making her stumble into a stool. "Hey Daxy! Looking damned sexy tonight." He nudged Dax's arm.

"Ahh!" Dax clutched his midsection. "Dude, what the fuck? You can't just pound me like that."

"Come on, I barely touched you. Stop being such a pussy." Finn nodded at Sara. "And now your old lady is gonna kick my ass, right?"

She glowered at Finn and grazed Daxton's arm. "Seriously, Finn? You know he's still healing. Any little jolt will hurt like hell!"

All the color disappeared from Finn's face. "Dax, man, I'm sorry. I didn't know it was still that bad. You've been so much more active lately."

"You're such a jerk, Finn!" She touched the bandages under Daxton's starched white shirt. "Are you okay? Do you want to sit down?"

Daxton winked at her. "I'm good. I promise. I'm just fucking with him."

"You're a real dickhead, man."

"Have some respect for the injured. Have you ever taken a knife to the chest? Had it slice up your insides like Carpaccio?"

Finn drained the rest of his beer. "Still scrounging around for the sympathy votes, huh? It hasn't gotten old yet?"

Time could never erase the image of Daxton lying unconscious on the floor of his green room, in a pool of his own blood. After all they'd been through, the knowledge that she might lose him was crushing. Nightmares haunted her every time she closed her eyes, and would continue to do so until whoever did this was locked up behind bars. Better yet, *dead*. He was lucky the knife had missed his heart, but it did plenty of damage to his stomach and lungs. God, it could have been so much worse. And it wasn't over yet. The sicko who'd done it would be back. Deep down, she knew it. And next time, would they be as fortunate?

"You know he's just trying to get a rise out of you," Daxton whispered. "He's jealous I have my own personal nurse, who likes to dress up in those sexy little outfits and take care of my *needs*."

"Or maybe I just want you to stop wallowing and get back into the studio so we can finish recording the next album."

Cooper stumbled over, tripping into Sara, a near-empty highball glass clutched in his hand. "I always knew she was a dangerous one. Kick his ass, Sara."

She snickered. "Sorry? I didn't catch that through the slurring."

"Just trying to have a good time. It's been a long few months."

"Have you heard from Laney?" Sara lowered her voice, but based on Cooper's level of intoxication, the answer was pretty clear.

"Nope." A grimace shadowed his face, his bloodshot eyes narrowing. "It was a mistake. I never should have started anything."

"Coop." Sara furrowed her brow. "I'm sorry."

He shrugged. "We just didn't fit. Fuck her."

Laney still hadn't returned from her trip off the deep end following Gia's accident. Her career was crumbling, band members displaced, her livelihood in a shambles. For a guy like Cooper, who already had his own demons hot on his heels, she wasn't the ideal mate. And the crash was devastating to watch.

"You know the right girl is out there." Sara squeezed his hand. Saying too much was almost as bad as keeping quiet. The last thing she wanted to do was tear open old wounds and douse them with salt, but the guy was a catastrophe waiting to happen. He needed help, not more booze.

"Maybe…" His voice trailed off and he slammed his glass on the bar. "Another, please. Make it a double."

"Coop." Dax's eyebrows furrowed. "Maybe you should go easy tonight."

"Dude, I don't need a lecture. Let the wifey look out for *you*. I'm good."

The hell he was.

Merrick appeared behind Daxton, his normally spiked blue hair slicked back. "You look good, man. How are you feeling?"

"Can't complain. I'm getting daily sponge baths from my hot little nurse, complete with happy endings."

A hot flush heated Sara's neck, traveling to her cheeks. These guys were like brothers, but still, they didn't need those types of details.

Merrick stiffened and clinked the ice cubes in his empty glass. "Great. I'm glad to hear you're on the mend."

"You know, I still don't get how that crazy motherfucker

managed to escape without a trace. There were no prints left on the weapon, no eyewitnesses. Nada. Merrick, you really didn't see anything?" Finn drained the rest of his beer.

Merrick's shoulders hunched, and he averted his eyes. "You guys already heard the story. I told the police everything I know. I was in the bathroom, and the noise must have startled the perp. I didn't even know Dax was in there until Sara showed up."

Wait, what? "But Merrick, the lights were on when Sean and I got there. And I thought you told the police you'd come into the room to find your phone." That in itself had been a little hard to swallow, considering the guy's device was permanently glued to his hand. Not that they would have any reason to doubt him, since he was Daxton's best friend, but why was the story changing now?

He ran a hand through his hair, his eyes flashing. "Look, I was bleeding and dizzy as hell. Maybe I flipped on the light before I collapsed. I told you, I didn't see anything."

"Yeah, but then why didn't you call for help? You must have seen Dax. Why would you have left him?" Sara's fists clenched. And what was this about the bathroom? That wasn't something he'd ever told them. Or had he? Jesus, she'd been so consumed with panic that night. Was it possible she misunderstood? Or was she just going nuts?

Daxton wrapped an arm around her waist. "Babe, stop. It's over. You know Merrick was behind the couch when he was attacked. He wouldn't have seen me."

She took a deep breath, stomach churning. That gruesome imagery was forever branded into her memory. "You're right. I'm sorry, I just…can we *not* talk about this anymore? Please?"

"Yeah, I think it's time for another round. Who else needs one?" Cooper's words were even more slurred, if that was possible.

"Cooper, why don't you and the guys grab seats at the table where Liam is sitting? I'll get the next round."

Cooper let out a loud snort. "I'm perfectly capable of getting my own drink, Sara."

Yeah, too bad you're not able to stand.

"You can get the next one." She shook her head at Daxton. Jeez, were they going to need an intervention? Cooper was in a downward spiral, and they had to figure out a way to pull him out before it sucked him in permanently.

Cooper slinked toward the table, grumbling with each step. Sara expelled a long, unsteady breath. At least he wouldn't be off banging cocktail waitresses or bridesmaids. Not that he hadn't tried.

She twisted toward the bar, a loud gasp escaping her lips. "Merrick! I didn't see you standing there. Why didn't you go with the others? I can handle this."

His eyes darkened for a split second, so fast, it was almost as if she'd imagined it. "I figured you could use a hand. Come on, there's another bar in the guesthouse. It'll be faster than waiting for one of the waitresses."

"Good idea." She linked her arm with his, feeling his body tense against her. The guy was moody as hell, even more so over the past couple of months, but she'd chalked it up to the stalker still being on the loose. Everyone was on edge, including her, since there were absolutely no leads. It didn't seem possible, but the attacker had escaped without a trace. She darted her eyes around the expansive grounds. Tyler spared no expense for security. Nobody was getting beyond that armed beefcake barrier.

A canopy of white fabric blanketed the outdoor bar, tulle wrapped in soft white lights winding down the spindles. Her heels clicked on the hardwood floor as she scurried toward an empty space in the corner. Perfect. She could slip right in and snag the attention of the bartender-slash-model checking himself out in the cocktail shaker.

A strong hand gripped her shoulder. "Inside," Merrick mumbled. "It'll take forever out here."

"But there's a spot right over—"

"Trust me, it's better if we go inside. They keep the better stuff out of the heat."

For such a long time, she'd turned herself inside out to get on Merrick's good side. Sometimes, it just wasn't worth it to argue. Air-conditioned booze? Lead the way.

After a short walk behind the gardens, she grasped the brass handle and pushed open a large, white door leading into the guesthouse, squinting so her eyes would adjust to the darkness. "Merrick, are you sure this is the indoor bar? I don't think there's anyone in he—"

A large hand clapped over her mouth, Merrick's large silver ring clanging against her tooth. Her pulse throbbed in her throat. Oh God, what was happening?

He shoved her against a wall with his hulking body, one hand still pressed to her lips, one hand slowly closing around her throat. The sound of shattering glass around her sent chills zipping down her spine. Her eyes struggled to adjust, but there was not even a single sliver of light in the room. No refuge from the ominous darkness that consumed her and swallowed her whole. Breaths became shallow as her airway tightened in his vise-like grip. *No oxygen... can't breathe...* Her limbs morphed into wet noodles, a clanging noise reverberating between her ears. Nobody would find her in time, even if she could manage to squeak out a single syllable. An icy sensation assaulted her fingertips, shooting up her arms and down her legs. Each passing second guided her closer to her last.

"Those other whores were so easy to handle, but you?" His grip around her neck loosened. "You kept slipping through my fingers. Not anymore. No, I finally have you right where I want you." He let go of her throat and reached into his pocket.

Tears blurred her vision. It had been *Merrick*? But why? Her body quaked with silent sobs, mind foggy with confusion.

"He was never yours, Sara. He was always mine." The stale stench of scotch made her stomach roll. He bit off a piece of gray duct tape and slapped it over her mouth.

Oh my God, oh my God, oh my God. This can't be happening.

Merrick leaned closer, his bright blue eyes darkening, filled with malice, his voice dripping with disdain. "Yeah, you're finally getting it, aren't you? I know you're from Podunk, Middle America, but you're no moron. Your dipshit boyfriend Eli told me just enough about your past. All I needed to do was fill in the blanks. Thanks to Google, that wasn't too hard. And guess what else? I'm not willing to share. You've already taken too much." He held up a syringe and flicked the needle with his finger. "So I need to get rid of you, and I'm gonna watch you suffer for every time you fucked Dax, before your body finally gives up. Just like you watched your dumbass druggie boyfriend drown in that lake. How's that for poetic justice?"

The sun dipped low on the horizon, an orange glow settling over the grandiose white silk tents. Tyler and Layla graced the dance floor, unable to keep their hands - or mouths - off one another from one second to the next, acting more like horny teenagers than adults. Well, at least Tyler was an adult. The verdict was still out on his wife. There had been lots of speculation on her actual age, but no confirmation. With that stripper body, she'd no doubt keep him sated, that was for sure.

Cooper tapped the face of his watch. "Hey, where the hell did Sara go for those drinks? I'm losing my buzz."

Daxton scanned the crowd, desperate to shrug off the feeling of unease that had settled into his conscious. Every time Sara disappeared from sight, panic overtook, the knowledge that some crazy stalker was still out there, lurking patiently for the next opportunity to pounce and inflict harm on her. But saying anything would only give credence to her fears, and the last thing he wanted was to see her in distress. Dammit, he should have made Sean follow her. Fuck normalcy. A couple of months ago, things were different. But now, they were living in a different time; a time where sick fuckers wouldn't rest until their target was eliminated. "Maybe she had to make a pit stop." The evening air was cool, but the goose bumps popping up along his arms weren't caused by the drop in temperature. Enough time had passed. When his arms were wrapped around her, he'd be able to relax. Then, and only then. "Hey, I'm going to run to the guesthouse for my guitar. I left it in one of the bedrooms."

"Text Merrick. He'll get it for you. It's a long walk." Liam draped an arm around his girlfriend, Lacie's, shoulders, dropping a kiss on her bare skin.

"It's fine. I can walk a few feet, lazy ass." Daxton gripped the arms of the chair and lifted himself out, gritting his teeth. Still sore, but fuck it. He was alive.

Cooper slammed his hands on the table. "I'll come with, as long as we can make *my* kind of pit stop along the way."

"Great, and if I have to carry your sorry ass, who's gonna have my back?"

"You're looking mighty sexy tonight, brother. I'm sure someone will happily volunteer for the job."

Daxton rolled his eyes. "Let's move. You know Tyler hates to be kept waiting, and we have to do a quick sound check before we get on stage."

Crowds of wedding guests spilled into every available space on the dance floor. Pulse pounding beats vibrated the floor beneath his feet, the sounds almost loud enough to drown out all thought. A girl in a tight black bandage dress flashed a slow smile as he pushed Cooper past the bar. Her bright blue eyes sparkled with something a little more potent than just plain excitement, and the come-hith-er look wasn't wasted on her target audience.

"Oh fuck, yeah," Cooper mumbled under his breath. He grasped Daxton's shoulder. "Dude, why don't you go ahead without me? I think I'm ready to make that pit stop right about now."

"You're a real tool, you know that? We're supposed to perform in ten. Don't get lost under her dress for too long."

Cooper snickered. "Dress is like Saran Wrap. It ain't staying on long."

He watched Cooper saunter up to the silicone-en-hanced brunette, a smile tugging his lips upward. Whatever got his mind off Laney. Chick had gotten under his skin like…Christ, like only one other before her. Bad news. Wait, scratch that. Obscenely, horrifically, colossally, horri-bly, bad news. Fuck that. He couldn't watch Cooper tumble down that rabbit hole again.

Soft, white twinkling lights illuminated a path toward the guesthouse, and there was still no sign of Sara. Dusk had set in, and no other light shone from the windows. The place looked deserted. Why weren't any of the guards flank-ing entrances with their Uzis? The iron gates were a decent deterrent, but it wasn't like some sicko would have to scale barbed wire to get beyond the perimeter. Not like there were attack dogs patrolling the property, although he'd have paid a shitload for a canine contingent. He pressed his fingers to his temples, his feet pounding the cobblestones. Fuck! Why did he let her go alone?

He reached the closest door, breathless, the windows completely black. A loud crash from inside the house made him jump. He stumbled backward into a large bush, grabbing onto the branches to keep from falling into the dirt. Needles pricked his exposed skin, but it was better than face planting into the flowerbed. A quick scan of the grounds confirmed he was still alone. His pulse throbbed, fuzzy memories of the attack looping through his mind. Logic crept into his conscious. *Go back to the reception, find security, don't open the door.*

But his hand ignored the persistent voices. The only thing driving him was Sara. He grasped the brass handle, the heavy door creaking open, blanketing him in darkness. His chest tightened, unsure of what he was about to find, hoping it was just one of Layla's cats knocking into a vase. But the icy sensation slithering down his spine told a different story.

His trembling fingers found the wall switch and slid it upward. "Sara?" No response. Nothing but eerie silence. He crept toward the nearest hallway, avoiding the porcelain chunks scattered across the marble tile floor. No cat in sight.

Get help!

Find Sara!

Call Sean!

Competing thoughts rang between his ears, all reason flying out the still-open door. Someone was in the house with him. He felt it.

Click, click, click.

Daxton's stomach clenched at the intruding sound, his fingers closing around a nearby brass lamp stand. He pulled his arm back, prepared to strike. His muscles tensed, grip tight. Fucking lamp was heavy, and he'd make sure it did enough damage to stop whoever the hell was terrorizing them.

A shadow from one of the rooms appeared on the shiny tile floor, slowly getting larger as it approached.

Click, click, click.

"Dax." Merrick appeared from a nearby doorway. He looked like shit, rumpled, sweaty, completely opposite his normal coiffed self. "You came."

All the breath vacated his body. He collapsed against the wall and dropped the lamp stand. "Q, what the fuck are you doing in here in the dark? I thought you were that crazy stalker."

Merrick ran a hand down over his face. "You shouldn't be here."

Daxton's eyes widened. Blood spotted the front of Merrick's white shirt. "Are you hurt? Why is there blood on your shirt?" His temples pounded. "Where is Sara?"

"Did you really not know, Dax?" Merrick inched closer. His voice was flat, blue eyes void of any emotion, dull, lifeless.

"Not know what? What the hell are you talk—?"

Merrick's lips stretched into a straight tight line. "For years I've done everything to show you how I feel. Is it because you just don't care? Is that why you ignored all my attempts?"

The words kept coming out, but Daxton's mind was unable to formulate questions. The air was so humid, yet the chills persisted. "Merrick, I don't understand what you're talking about. What have you tried to show me?"

"You called me Merrick," he mused, raking his hands through his blue-tipped hair, creeping closer. "You haven't called me that in years."

"I feel like I'm missing something. You're my best friend. If I did something to piss you off, just tell me." Daxton's pulse spiked under Merrick's penetrating gaze.

"Your friendship isn't enough, Dax. I need...no I *crave*, all of you. I can't fight it anymore. For years, I've watched you parade around those groupie sluts." Merrick circled him, his stare transforming into something decidedly more predatory. His temples throbbed, blood rushing between his ears. "Every time I got rid of one, another would show up, flashing her tight, shiny pussy at you."

Beads of perspiration popped up along the back of Daxton's neck, almost as though his body had lapped his mind in the quest for clarity. "Got rid of who, Merrick?"

"All of them. Brandi, Gia... Sara." His blue eyes darkened, his voice gruff. "I had to eliminate the competition."

"Merrick, what have you done to Sara?"

His shoulders hunched forward. "I knew you'd never fall in love with me if she were still around. Not that she could ever give you what you need. Not like I could."

"You sick fuck!" Daxton grabbed the lapels of Merrick's tuxedo jacket and threw him against a wall. The force sent a row of paintings crashing to the marble floor. "What did you do?"

"It's too late to worry about what I did. She can't have you because you're mine." A smile tugged at the corners of Merrick's mouth. "And also because she's dead. Well, at least close to it."

Dead... dead... dead.

The word thundered between Daxton's ears. His clenched fist crashed against Merrick's mouth, but that sinister smile never fucking wavered. Again and again, he pounded with everything he had, ignoring the pain slicing through his chest with each launch of his arm.

Merrick finally crumbled to the floor, blood gushing from his nose and lips. "You're too late, Dax. If I can't have you, neither can she."

Daxton fell to his knees, his eyes stinging with tears. "You sonofabitch!" He fisted Merrick's short, spiky hair and slammed his head backward into the wall. "Sara!" He struggled to his feet, his voice echoing throughout the vacant guesthouse as he stumbled down the hallway. One of the bedroom doors was cracked open, a dim light shining into the otherwise darkened space. He pushed open the door, a strangled cry escaping his mouth.

"Sara," he whispered, crossing the room in a few short steps. Duct tape covered her mouth, an IV needle stuck out of her blotchy, red arm. His eyes fell to the clear bag of liquid at her side. Potassium chloride. He collapsed next to her limp body, grasping her cold, almost lifeless fingers. Her eyes fluttered open, bloodshot and swollen.

His fingers trembled as he pulled the tape off the needle. Sara barely winced. There wasn't time to wait for a medic. Whatever the hell poison this was had to—

"Dax! Are you ready or what? Coop said you came back here for your guitar." Finn's booming voice broke the silence in the guesthouse. "Jesus Christ! What happened in here?"

"Finn! I'm in the bedroom. Get help!"

Finn's footsteps pounded on the tile floor as he approached. "Holy shit! Who the hell did this?"

"It was Merrick. He has her hooked up to a potassium chloride drip. I don't know how long it's been, but we need help. Get a medic!" He grabbed a bunch of tissues from a nearby table, pressed them to the swollen area on her arm and slid out the needle.

"Merrick? Get the fuck out of here! Did you see him? Where is he?"

Daxton's stomach dropped to his knees. "What do you mean? I knocked him out. He's in the foyer."

"Only thing in the foyer is a whole lotta blood, dude. No Merrick." Finn pulled out his phone and shot off a quick call. "Okay, Sean and the medic are on the way. Is she conscious?"

Tears stung Daxton's eyes. He pulled off the duct tape and pressed his lips to Sara's. "Baby, can you hear me?"

Her eyes opened a crack then closed again. Breathing was steady, that had to be a good sign. "Brandi and Gia," she mumbled.

He let out a relieved breath. Thank God she could speak. "What about them?"

"It was Merrick. Said I didn't deserve you, that only he could satisfy you." She shifted, letting out a low groan. "My arm really hurts."

"What the hell, man?" Finn whispered. "Is she hallucinating or something?"

Daxton shook his head and caressed the side of her face. "No."

"He's in love with Dax," Sara murmured, her eyes closing again.

"Stay with me, baby." Dax squeezed her hands. "You're gonna be fine. Just keep those gorgeous eyes open."

"So Merrick is gay? The guy who bangs more chicks than all of us put together? Holy fuck, that's a lot to process." Finn raked a hand through his hair.

Loud sirens approached, the piercing noises resounding in the guesthouse. Footsteps pounded into the foyer, walkie-talkies blaring.

"Dax! Where you at?"

Never had he been so happy to hear Sean's voice. "We're in here!"

A throng of people descended upon them. One of the medics knelt down, checking Sara's vitals. "Tell me what happened."

Daxton managed to recount what he'd found above the din of voices. "I don't know how long the needle was in, but she's been semi-conscious. Maybe she didn't get that much from the drip."

The medic pointed to the injection site. "Nope. This is a case of pure luck. You see all this swelling? It means whoever set up the IV blew the vein. The needle may have been too big, or it was just inserted incorrectly. It ruptured, meaning the potassium chloride spilled into the surrounding area. Anything injected would just be absorbed into her body."

"So she's fine?"

"We'll run some blood work, but judging from the amount of liquid still in the bag, I'd say yes."

"Dax!" Tyler pushed through the small crowd that had formed in the bedroom. "What the hell is going on? Is everyone okay?"

Daxton let out a deep sigh, still gripping Sara's hand as the medics loaded her onto a stretcher. "For the moment."

"Merrick tried to kill Sara," Finn offered.

Tyler's eyes looked like they were going to pop out of his head. "Merrick?"

"Stabbed Dax, too. But that was an accident. He thought it was Sara. Tonight he came to finish the job, but he botched it all up."

Tyler's mouth dropped open. "But why?"

"Apparently, he has the hots for your son and in his deluded blue-tipped head, he thought if he offed Sara, they'd be able to run off into the sunset together."

Tyler rubbed his temples. "Where the hell is he now?"

"Don't worry, Mr. Cole. We're sealing off the perimeter. We'll get him." Sean palmed the walkie-talkie in his hand and exited the room, barking instructions to the security team.

Tyler clapped a hand on the medic's shoulder. "Just tell me Sara is going to be okay."

"Her vitals are strong and steady." The medic smiled. "We've got it from here."

"Dad, I'm going to the hospital. Tell Layla I'm really sorry."

"Hey!" Tyler grabbed Daxton and hugged him tight. "Take care of your girl, and call me later. Don't worry about Layla. I've got plenty to keep her happy and thoroughly occupied."

Daxton mustered up the energy to flash a quick smirk. "I don't need to hear any more about that, thank you very much."

"I'm coming with you." Finn slung an arm around Daxton's shoulders. "Someone has to protect you from your scorned lover."

"You know, you joke, but that crazy bastard got away. He's still out there."

"They'll find him, man. He won't stay away, trust me. Your ass is too hot. He won't be able to help himself."

"You're a real dickhead."

Outside the guesthouse, a team of medics loaded Sara's stretcher into an ambulance. Throngs of wedding guests spilled onto the lawn, watching the emergency medical team at work. Sean had dispersed the security team over the property in search of Merrick. Nobody had anticipated he'd stick close to the strike zone, at least nobody other than Finn.

Crack!

A large terra cotta planter a few feet from the ambulance shattered into pieces as the bullet tore through it. Screams resonated as people fell to the ground to take cover.

Finn pulled Daxton to the grass as a window shattered behind them.

"Let me go! Sara!" Daxton struggled to his feet. The ambulance door was still open. The shots were getting closer. He stumbled toward the vehicle, falling against the doors. Sweat drizzled down his back, soaking his shirt. The only thing that mattered was keeping Sara safe. Hell, he'd give his life for hers in a hot second.

"You betrayed me, Dax!" Merrick's voice carried over the grounds. Daxton's eyes scoured the expanse, searching for Merrick, but all he saw were tuxedos and ball gowns scattered on the grass. "You chose her over me. I loved you so much, and you never even noticed! You destroyed me, Dax. My life is nothing without you, and if I can't have you, nobody can!"

Pop!

Daxton fell against the ambulance as another planter shattered. "Get the hell out of here!" he shouted to the driver and slammed the doors shut.

The engine roared to life and the tires peeled away, headed down the hidden driveway.

"I can't watch you with her anymore, Dax." Merrick emerged from the shadows, his face twisted into a grimace. "You may have saved her this time, but you can't save yourself. And me?" He raised his arm, pointing the gun at Daxton's chest. "I'm already dead."

"Drop the gun, you mother fucker!" Cooper's voice rang into the air. He hurled himself at Merrick, knocking him against the stucco wall of the guesthouse, the gun still tight in his grip.

"Get the fuck off me, Cooper!" Merrick smashed the gun against Cooper's jaw, but it wasn't enough to slow him down. Cooper pounded his fist into Merrick's throat and then into his temple.

Daxton ran toward the struggle. His leg muscles were so tense; it was a miracle he could even move.

"Dax, get back!" Sean grabbed his arm and yanked him to the ground. Sharp pains sliced through his abdomen as if they were machetes. "Ahh! Goddammit, Sean!" He twisted out of Sean's grip and struggled to pull himself up. "I have to help Co—"

Pop! Crack! Bang!

An explosion of bullets shattered his eardrums, the lingering echo ricocheting through him as he pitched forward onto the dewy grass. Blinding white light flooded his periphery, the putrid stench of chemicals stinging his nostrils. Searing heat singed his insides, numbness creeping along in its wake. Daxton lay in a crumpled heap; the ability to move, to *breathe,* slowly escaped. A sharp breath lodged in his throat, eyes struggling to focus, waiting and praying for the mercy that might never be granted. His heart skidded to a stop. He choked on the scream forming in his throat, but his lungs couldn't grasp the air to push it out. *Please, God, no.*

Merrick didn't move. Neither did Cooper.

Six Months Later…

LIGHTS IN THE SPACIOUS BALLROOM dimmed, a spotlight focused on the life-sized photo behind the podium. Daxton gazed into the bright, blue eyes of his beloved brother. He swallowed past the golf-ball sized lump in his throat that always seemed to lodge itself there when he saw the image of Jase's smiling face, before he'd gotten sick. Before the cancer consumed him and claimed his young life.

A hush fell over the crowd as Daxton adjusted the microphone. "This is my brother, Jason Cole. He died eighteen months ago of inoperable brain cancer. He was only eighteen." A painful ache took up residence in his heart, his eyes falling to the table right in front of the stage, filled with the most important people to him. Sara's eyes glistened with unshed tears, her hands entwined with Tyler's. Finn and Liam sat on either side of them. But one seat was empty...glaringly so. A pang in his chest served as a warning, a red flag that could no longer be ignored. "Tonight, we come together to celebrate his memory, and the memories of other children who've succumbed to terminal illnesses. The Jason T. Cole Foundation was established to provide financial support to the families of these afflicted kids, so they can focus their energy on making memories, instead of worrying about medical bills."

Daxton scanned the faces in the darkened room. His lips curled into a small smile as his gaze connected with Luke's parents, their tearful expressions illuminated by the soft candlelight of the centerpiece. It had been eight months since Luke's passing, and that was one of the main reasons why he'd started the foundation. Too many young lives had been lost due to this devastating disease, too many families burdened with financial difficulties because of it. Taking Sara's advice, he'd decided it was time to raise awareness with the public and help ease the trauma these families experienced. "I'd like to thank you all for being here tonight for our first benefit. Your generous donations will bring a great deal of comfort to so many families, and we are very grateful for your support. Together, we can make a difference in the lives of these families, bringing them comfort at a time when they feel like all hope is lost. Thank you for being part of our mission."

He turned away from the podium amid the thunderous applause, casting a final glance at Jase's photo. "Check it out, buddy," he murmured, lifting his pant legs to reveal one purple dress sock and one blue and white striped mismatch. "Your favorite non-pair."

Sara, Tyler, and the guys stood up when he rejoined them at the table. Still no Cooper. He wrapped his arms around Sara's lithe frame and squeezed tightly, burying his head into the smooth skin of her neck.

"Are you okay?" she whispered.

"I am now." He pulled back to brush his lips against hers before giving Tyler a quick hug.

Finn clapped him on the back. "He's right here with us, buddy."

"Always." Liam nodded, a somber expression on his face.

"Where's Coop?"

The guys exchanged a look. The same concern reflected in their gazes. "He's at the bar with Laney."

"This has been really hard for him. It's tearing open the old wounds," Finn murmured. "He was good for a while, but Laney..."

Daxton ran a hand through his slicked back hair. It hadn't been the easiest six months. Layla evidently didn't subscribe to the belief that a shootout at your first wedding was a harbinger of good things to come, and she'd taken off only a few months after gushing her "I dos" to Tyler. Gold digging bitch. Then he'd had to deal with burying Merrick, his former best friend turned psychopath. Cooper's downward spiral after the wedding attack that they'd both miraculously escaped unscathed. Luke's untimely death...God, there had been so much loss and devastation surrounding him. The foundation provided the anchor he'd needed to remain grounded, hopeful, and focused on the future.

But Cooper had let go of his anchor and was now floating off into the abyss. A rescue fleet couldn't save him. Daxton let out a deep sigh. They couldn't lose Cooper, too, but dammit, he was almost out of reach. The one person who could have pulled him back was the one person who'd ended up driving him further away. *Damn you, Laney.*

"I'm so proud of you," Tyler said, his voice cracking.

"You're doing a really special thing here."

"Thanks, Dad. That means more than you know." Amazing how only a few words could have such a big impact. Christ, they'd wasted so much time, but the regrets that littered his past were way too many in number to count. Looking forward was his priority. Getting lost in the past, and succumbing to the disappointment over things beyond his control…that part of his life was over. It was time to start a new chapter, and this was the perfect occasion. Well, almost.

"Go talk to him," Sara whispered. "I'll be here when you get back."

He brushed his lips against hers. "Have I told you how lucky I am to have you?"

"Only about five times today. But don't worry, I'll let you tell me again later." With a wink, she nudged him. "Go."

It wasn't hard to spot Cooper at the bar in the back of the banquet room, hunched over in a corner with a few empty shot glasses lined up on the shiny mahogany wood. "What happened to you, man?"

Cooper looked up, his expression vacant, distant, just…

lost. It was a shitty place to be; something Daxton knew all too well. But he'd been lucky enough to find someone who believed in him enough to bring him back from the edge. Who was going to save Cooper from being swallowed up by the regret and the despair that clouded him?

"Laney left."

"Again?"

"Yep." Cooper lifted a full shot glass to his lips.

"Maybe that's not such a bad thing." Treading lightly was a must. Cooper's pupils looked like saucers, and too many words would send him spiraling into the unknown.

"Stay out of my fucking business, Dax." He downed the amber-colored liquid and slammed the glass on the bar. "You think you get the right to judge because you're living the fairy tale?" His speech was slurred, courtesy of the liquor, combined with whatever the hell he'd popped or smoked.

"She's not good for you, Coop. You know it as well as I do. You're in a bad place right now, I get it. But you need to walk away. I'm afraid she'll drag you back to—"

"Drag me back where? To the place where my life is complete shit? Guess what? I'm already there."

"You need help, Coop. Please don't push everyone away. Let us help you through this."

"I don't want anything from you. I'm not your next charity case. You take care of your own life and stay out of mine." He pushed away from the bar and struggled to his feet.

"Look, you should get some rest. Let me call a car." Daxton gripped his shoulder to steady him.

Cooper shook off his hand. "I have a phone." He pulled it from his pocket, stumbling into a nearby table in the process. "See?"

"Hey, man. I think it's time to call it a night. Car's here." Finn's approaching voice sliced through the tension looming in the air.

Cooper let out a loud snort. "Guess you're the babysitter tonight, huh?" He rolled his eyes, slinking toward the exit. "Do I get a snack before bed if I'm a good boy?"

"Thanks, Finn," Daxton murmured. The drugs and the alcohol turned Cooper into a guy he didn't know; a guy he didn't *want* to know, truth be told. And that made it damned hard to want to help him when all he did was push away with his scalding rhetoric. "He's in bad shape. He said some pretty shitty stuff."

"Stop. You know how he gets when this crap with Laney hits. Let him sleep it off. We'll deal with it tomorrow. Enjoy tonight. You guys deserve it." Finn punched him in the shoulder. "Don't stay up all night celebrating. We're meeting at the studio at nine. The new manager is supposed to show up, too."

"Don't worry about me. Just make sure Cooper sobers up by then."

"On it. Now you get on it." Finn snickered as he sauntered out of the bar in pursuit of a staggering, belligerent Cooper.

Daxton walked over to where Sara was waiting and grasped her hands. She was so beautiful, so perfect, inside and out, a true beacon of light whose rays never faltered. He was going to make sure she heard those words every day for the rest of her life. The rest of *their* lives.

"How is Cooper?" She bit her lower lip. "What happened with Laney?"

"Same shit, different day. I wish she'd stay the hell away from him. He was finally getting over the hump, and she sent him reeling back into the past."

"You can't live his life, Dax. He has to want to get better."

"I know. I've tried so many times, but it's no use. The further away he gets, the more I think he'll never come back." He shook his head. "And tonight, the tribute to Jase…"

"It hasn't been easy for him. You know that. Give him some time. He'll come around."

"I hope you're right."

"I hope so, too."

He curled a loose tendril of her hair around his finger. "Take a walk with me."

"And disappoint your public?" She smirked, waving her hand around. "There are a lot of people here looking to corner the most devastatingly handsome philanthropist in the room. How do you expect to escape unnoticed?"

"I know how to fly under the radar."

"Yeah, thanks to my expert publicity guidance." She giggled. "Glad you finally paid attention."

He snaked an arm around her slim waist and led her to a set of tall glass doors. They stepped out into the cool night air, the sky brightened by a blanket of stars. Moonlight danced atop her soft, silky blonde hair. It looked like spun gold skimming her bare shoulders. "You're breathtaking."

Her face relaxed into a smile. "You're biased."

"No, I just love you." He tightened his grip, pulling her closer.

"I love you, too." She let out a deep sigh and rested her face against his neck.

Sara had been more relaxed and settled over the past few months than he'd ever seen her. After so much time had passed, she and her parents had finally reconciled and begun to work through their issues. Daxton had always encouraged her to reach out to them, but in the end, it was Sara's mother who initiated the contact. Ever since then, they'd made several trips back to Minnesota. And after their latest visit, he'd received several anxious phone calls from her parents. Tonight, he and Sara would be the ones making the call with the exciting news they'd been waiting to hear.

"So, you've gone from being my publicist to my girlfriend to my foundation co-founder. Some progression, huh?"

"It's been a fun ride." She snickered. "You know, for the most part."

"Yeah, aside from being stabbed, shot at, injected with poison…"

"I never expected a rose garden."

"But you deserve one."

"That's very sweet, but I'm actually allergic."

"I think I can come up with an acceptable substitute." He stroked the back of her head, the shiny strands so smooth against his fingers.

"Oh yeah?"

"Yeah." He reached into his pocket and pulled out the

grape-flavored ring pop that had been burning a hole in his pocket since he'd picked it up from the store earlier that day. "You believed in me when nobody else did, Sara. You inspired me to get my life in order, to find purpose and meaning, and to look forward instead of choking on the past."

Sara's mouth dropped open. "Dax?"

He fell to his knee on the cobblestone path. "Everything was dark before you plowed into me that night in Houston. And ever since then, you've been my bright and shiny, the one sparkling star in a world of gray. You're my best friend, my everything. Marry me, Sara. Be my wife. Give me the chance to make you as happy as you've made me...forever."

Her large eyes shone in the moonlight, pooling with tears as she spoke the single word he longed to hear, "Yes!"

"So this makes it official, right? No more threat of tourmance?"

A giggle escaped her lips and she sniffed. "I think we're beyond that hurdle. But what happens when I finish sucking on this delicious ring pop?" She smirked. "Is there a substitute for that, too?"

"Oh, I can definitely find other things for you to suck. But you're right, it won't last forever. Not like this one." He pulled out a tiny velvet Harry Winston box and popped open the top.

"Or like us." Her eyes sparkled as bright as the tiny facets on the five-carat. "It's gorgeous," she breathed.

"Not as tasty as the first one, though."

"Not as sticky either." She wrapped her arms around his waist.

"Good thing I had a backup handy. I wouldn't want any competition for that mouth of yours."

"Just wait until we get home. My mouth has exciting plans for you."

"Do they involve the grape ice pops in the freezer?"

"Well, I know you prefer cherry, and I can be flexible."

Her teasing tone made his cock twitch. Drizzling fruit juices on his skin, having that greedy tongue mop up the sugary sweetness, tasting those lips in every sense of the word. The countdown to when they could slip away unnoticed had begun. "I like where this is heading."

"To the shower?"

He smiled, stroking the side of her face. "To forever."

THE END

ABOUT KRISTEN LUCIANI

Kristen Luciani is a self-proclaimed momtrepreneur with a penchant for Christian Louboutins, Silicon Valley, plunging necklines and grapefruit martinis. As a deep-rooted romantic who prefers juicy drama to fill the lives of anyone other than her, she tried her hand at creating a world of enchantment, sensuality, and intrigue, finally uncovering her true passion. No pun intended…

Connect with Kristen

Author Website: www.KristenLuciani.com

Twitter: twitter.com/kristen_luciani

Facebook: http://on.fb.me/1Y87KjV

Instagram: @kristen_luciani

Sign Up For Kristen's VIP Reader List:
http://bit.ly/1C27Kbh

Join The Stiletto Click on Facebook:
http://on.fb.me/1NOm76t

Other Works by Kristen Luciani

The Venture Series

Unlikely Venture, Book One

Nothing Ventured, Book Two

Venture Forward, Book Three

Joint Venture, Book Four

About Rebecca Manuel

Rebecca Manuel, a.k.a. Becca the Bibliophile, is a lover of books, Fireball, Diet Dr. Pepper and Texas Trash Pie from Royers Roundtop Café. With a deep-rooted passion for the creative, she started the first independent short film company within the literary industry, charged with bringing book characters and plots to life via the Internet. She lives in Houston with her techie geek husband, two fabulous kids, and their menagerie of furry friends.

Connect With Rebecca

Facebook: www.facebook.com/BibliophileProductions

Twitter: twitter.com/becbibliophile

Instagram: @becbibliophile

Website:
www.beccathebibliophile.wixsite.com/biblioproduction

ACKNOWLEDGEMENTS

We are thrilled with our decision to collaborate on Plowed, and it has been such a rewarding journey, one that began in the lobby bar of the Marriott on the eve of Indies Invade Philly 2015. It takes a lot of trust between both parties to embark on such a path, as well as seriously thick skin, since brutal honesty is essential. And yes, sometimes it's very, very brutal.

To our fabulous Wattpad and Newsletter Subscribers—Thank you, our loyal Jimmy Sixx groupies! You've been on this crazy tour with us from the beginning, and your enthusiasm has fueled our passion for this story even more than we thought possible!

To The Stiletto Click and The Naughty Hangout—You've been so supportive of this project, and we love you for your constant pleas for more Dax!

To our families—We adore you, and thank you for your love, support, and understanding when we're knee-deep in conversation about *what happens next*.

Thank you so much, and enjoy the ride!

Love,
Kristen and Becca

Interested in a light sexy read? Keep reading to check out
Chapter 1 of M.D. Saperstein's newest release,
Naked Truth!

by: M.D. Saperstein

For more information, or information regarding subsidiary rights, please contact the author:
AuthorSaperstein@aol.com
OR
https://www.facebook.com/MdSapersteinAuthor
OR
http://www.AuthorMDS.com

Edited by: Megan Hershenson
Cover Design by: Bibliophile Productions

Printed in the United States of America
First Printing, April 2016
ISBN: 978-1530657483

-1-
PIKE

PROSTITUTION IS ILLEGAL IN FLORIDA. It's actually illegal in most states. But I live and work in the great Sunshine State, so that's all I'm really concerned about. Just the thought of it makes my skin crawl. Now, I know what you are thinking – that I am a total hypocrite. I take my clothes off for money. I shake what my mama gave me for the bacon. I exploit my moneymaker for the paper. I am a stripper. Well, maybe not a stripper, per se, but a male exotic dancer. That sounds better, right? It's all semantics. It doesn't really matter what you call me because by the end of the night, I am pretty much naked, surrounded by sloppy drunk, not so beautiful women, pawing at me and grabbing my junk. Are they all ugly and gross? No, I've seen my share of beauties, but no one that I want to take home with me. But I do it all for the dollar bills. Not even the Benjamins. A fucking Washington. Does that make me a prostitute? Shit, it's pretty damn close. Certainly an underpaid one.

Oh, and did I mention that everyone just assumes that I am gay? It's because I really don't get hard, isn't it? When you see something every day, it's just not so appealing.

When I first started stripping, I had no control. I would be a walking erection. And now, months later, grinding on a random woman's ass doesn't do it for me anymore. I wonder if this is how gynecologists feel about vaginas. You've seen one, you've seen them all? Plus, when your blood is pumping and the adrenaline is flowing, your blood doesn't necessarily rush to where it usually does. These days, it takes a lot to get my dick to stand at attention, not just any arbitrary fox. But if for some reason I do want wood, I can just pop a Viagra. At least that's what I've been told. I haven't done that, and I don't plan to. If I get hard, it's going to be because my dick wants to be. Not because I drugged it to be. Even so, the club manager keeps a supply behind the bar for us dancers.

Shit, where are my manners? Let me introduce myself. My name is Jordan Pike, but my friends call me Pike. I haven't been called Jordan since grade school. The only person who still calls me Jordan is my mom, but even she usually just goes with the standard "honey" or "sweetie." Unless I am in trouble. Then, it's Jordan Taylor Pike. My colleagues at my old job called me Pike as well. Here, at this joint, I go by JT. It's just easier than coming up with some dumbass stage name like "Pussy eating Pike." I also have no interest in anyone here knowing how to contact me when I leave. Cause I will leave. Soon, I hope. I really want to return to my old job immediately.

I used to live and work in North Miami Beach, and I absolutely loved it. White sandy beaches, gorgeous women, and a hopping nightlife. My family is there and I have a great set of buddies I like to hang with. I also got along great with my colleagues. I miss my old job. I also enjoyed steadier hours and less shady people. Okay, that's a total lie. I was pretty much on-call 24/7 and at the disposal of the boss man, and the people were sketchy as shit. Nevertheless, it was the life I chose - making a difference in peoples' lives - and I wouldn't change it for the world.

My boss needed me to straighten out things at this club down south, so he sent me here. Temporarily, I hope. South Miami. That's where I am now. And although things are similar - it's still Miami, obviously - it's a whole other level of gross. The people here are much more aggressive, the women so grabby. Their boundaries are blurred, and I am sure the booze has a lot to do with it. Worst of all, I have no fucking idea what they are saying most of the time. No hablo Español. At least not the crass shit they are asking me to do.

Unlike how it's portrayed in the movies, the life of a male exotic dancer isn't as glamorous as it seems. Okay, yeah, it's cool having all of the attention, but in the end, it is very lonely. I leave work every night, alone, to an empty apartment. I'm not really into bringing home clients, accepting hotel room keys, or doing any "side work." No bachelorette parties, no divorce parties, and definitely, no bachelor parties. I've heard way too many stories about guys getting mauled, bitten, and even burned. Drunk and horny is a dangerous combination to be dancing half-naked with no stage or bouncers to help keep boundaries. Some women don't like to hear "no" or don't think that you are seriously rejecting them.

And since this job is hopefully temporary, so is the

apartment I've rented. It's a studio apartment, which means that there is no designated bedroom. It's just one big room. No, I take that back. It's just one tiny room. With a kitchenette in the corner. That's right, shit's so tiny that there's not even enough room for a full-sized kitchen. In fact, there isn't a full-sized anything in this apartment - except me. I am definitely a full-sized man.

At 6'5", I am the tallest dancer at the club. Let's get the bullshit out of the way before I continue. No, I don't play basketball. Yes, it's true what is said about the size of a man's shoe. Okay? Can we move on? As I was saying, as muscular as I am, I am not the bulkiest. There is a mini-gym in the back of the club to help us get pumped up before we go on stage. Watching these other dickheads work out is entertainment enough, trying to bulk up as much as possible. They have no idea what they are doing and they certainly have no idea what the ladies like. When I worked up north – and by up north, of course I am referring to North Miami – we had a trainer there to make sure that we knew what we were doing. I wouldn't be surprised if these douches are juicing. Hmm, note to self, find out who would be willing to inject shit into their bodies for no good fucking reason.

Drugs are illegal in Florida, too. I know what I must sound like – insert whiney bitch voice here - but I like things done on the up and up. I need rules and boundaries. I require structure and discipline. Hence, I like laws. Codes to live by. And while I know that dancing blurs the line, I make sure every night I am here, whether I am on stage or doing a private lap dance, I do not cross the line. I may step on it, but never cross it.

But the best part of my job - the only part I look forward to, actually - is knowing that every Wednesday I get to go back to my old job, see my old buddies, and deposit all of these singles. What's so special about a trip to the bank? Um, hello! Have you seen that beautiful little lady behind the glass? Now that's class.

Gotta go, they are calling my name... "All you ladies love him, wish your men could move like him…the one… the only…the delicious…Jayyyyy Teeeee!"

violet

I look at the clock every thirty minutes. It has become a habit, almost involuntary at this point. As time counts down, I begin my routine: Run my fingers through my long strawberry blonde hair and bring it forward over my shoulders, reapply my lip-gloss, smooth down my clothes, and check my teeth.

Every Wednesday, 3:00 pm, like clockwork. He walks through the double glass doors, nods at Cliff, our security guard, and then weaves through the maze to get to the front of the line. He always wears slacks and a dress shirt, untucked, no tie. His sleeves are rolled halfway up his forearms. His sexy, sinewy forearms. They are lightly dusted with the same dark hair that resides atop the most gorgeous face I've ever seen. Oh, that face. It is always clean-shaven and never a strand of hair out of place. I zone out every time I see him. Imagining that he is here for me. Wondering what he does for a living, taking wild guesses in my head. I pray that he is single. Please be single. I always end each daydream zeroing in on that left ring finger. Still nothing, thank god.

He walks - no, swaggers - past my window and I get a soft breeze, the faintest smell wafting over me. I close my eyes and take a deep breath, trying to be subtle and not look like a stalker. If I could just figure out what he uses, I would buy it and spread it across my pillow every night. Okay, so maybe that's a little stalkerish. I then experience the briefest trip to heaven as I gaze into his piercing hazel eyes as he offers me a wink and a smile. My day is made. All of my senses are in overdrive and I know I must savor them all until I get to experience him all over again, next Wednesday. Fortunately, I get to relive this day repeatedly, any time I want…in my head, of course.

He continues past me and stops in front of the glass only a few feet away, but I can't keep my eyes off of him. I try to look busy.

"Hello, Susie," he greets my coworker with a smile. There it is…the dimple in his right cheek. How a muscle deformity could be so sexy is beyond me. I would do any-thing to lick it.

"Good afternoon, Mr. Taylor. How can I help you to-day?" she asks him.

I fiddle with some papers at my station, trying to dis-tract myself while his smooth voice washes over me. I wish today, like every other Wednesday, he would stop at my window. I also wish that Susie got sick so she would have to take the day off. That's pretty shitty of me, isn't it?

"Just the usual deposit," he croons.

Another customer comes in and walks up to my window. Mrs. Harlow, divorced, works in a plastic surgeon's office, which would explain all of the Botox in her face. Not that you need to know any of that stuff, just more useless information ingrained into my memory. I have no choice but to give her my full attention and take care of her banking needs. I am, after all, North Miami Bank's number one customer service provider. I see from the corner of my eye that he is wrapping up with Susie. She is flirting as usual and the smile on his face most likely means that he is eating it up. Plus, her being 5'8", blonde, with blue eyes, we are completely opposite, and I am assuming that she is just his type, given that he walks right past my open window every week. I am barely 5'3", on a good day, and although I am in fairly good shape, I inherited my mother's curves.

Don't get me wrong, I'm not a schlump by any means. In fact, I have a few customers that ask me out whenever they come in. I'm sure one or two of them are serious about getting my number, but I know the majority are just being flirtatious. Too bad none of them gives me butterflies or makes me want to do naughty things to them.

I complete my transaction as quickly as possible with Mrs. Harlow so that I can catch sight of his fantastic ass as he leaves.

"Have a nice day, Mr. Taylor," Susie wishes, wiggling her fingers at him.

"I plan to," he answers with a wry smile.

Mr. Taylor turns to walk toward the door, taking the same route as he always does. I plop down on my stool and sigh. Just as he reaches Cliff, he completely devastates me. He turns back toward me and gestures as though he is lifting his top hat toward me, bidding me adieu. I think I just peed a little.

"I hate your guts," I say to Susie in jest, even though deep down I kinda do really mean it.

She just laughs and shrugs. "What? I can't help it if he wants to make a deposit into my box."

"Shut up, you're gross," I tell her then slip my pinkie through a rubber band, wrap it around my thumb, and secure it to my pointer finger. I am totally my father's daughter.

I aim my rubber band gun at her, daring her to say another thing.

"And why does he always come in with hundreds of singles? Do you think he's a stripper or something?" she asks, and that breaks the straw.

I pull the trigger, her shoulder my intended target, but oops!

"Ouch! Bitch! You hit my boob!" she yells at me in the middle of the bank. So much for being professional.

"That'll teach you not to talk about my future baby daddy like that. Stripper my ass! There is no way. I'm thinking accountant or lawyer. Why else would he be so dressed up every time we see him?"

"Baby daddy? You're crazy, Vi. No offense, but that man never stops at your window to deposit anything into your sorry box," she reminds me.

"I know. Maybe he's just playing hard to get," I joke, trying to take the sting out of her comment. We both share a quick chuckle then get back to work. A line is starting to form, anyway.

By 5:00 pm, I am ready to clock out. As much as I enjoy seeing that delicious man, it is stressful at the same time. I wish I had my sister's balls, but sadly, my inexperience with men and shyness continues to trip me up. One day.